Advance Praise for *The*

"Regina McBride evokes the splendors of landscapes and the exquisite textures of daily life in prose that adds luster and resonance to this book's vivid, compelling story."
—Maureen Dezell, author of *Irish America: Coming into Clover*

Praise for *The Nature of Water and Air*

"In her first novel, Regina McBride writes in a shimmering and hypnotic prose style. . . . The story builds like a fugue. *The Nature of Water and Air* has an urgent melancholy about it—it casts an undeniable spell."
—Emily White, *The New York Times Book Review*

"With its brooding Irish backdrop, lyrical language, and shrouded secrets, *The Nature of Water and Air* is a modern myth. Bottom line: This saga casts a spell."
—Christina Cheakalos, *People*

"Finely wrought and deeply felt, the novel is a work of supercharged imagination, in which the presence of sea spirits, ghosts, and the dire workings of fate contribute to an atmosphere of brooding mystery."
—*Publishers Weekly*

"What distinguishes *The Nature of Water and Air* . . . is the precision of the language and the haunting power of the narrative."
—Edna O'Brien

"*The Nature of Water and Air* is an astoundingly rich and lyrical novel about mothers and daughters, secrets and delusions, and the salve of love. . . . Maeve Binchy, Roddy Doyle, Regina McBride is your peer."
—Tillie Olsen

"Lyrical and sad, infused with fascinating folklore and the chill of the Irish landscape. A literary Maeve Binchy."
—Beth Gibbs, *Library Journal*

The Land of Women

A NOVEL

REGINA McBRIDE

A Touchstone Book

PUBLISHED BY SIMON & SCHUSTER

NEW YORK LONDON TORONTO SYDNEY SINGAPORE

TOUCHSTONE
Simon & Schuster, Inc.
Rockefeller Center
1230 Avenue of the Americas
New York, NY 10020

For information about special discounts for bulk purchases, please contact Simon & Schuster Special Sales: 1-800-456-6798 or business@simonandschuster.com

Designed by Colin Joh
Text set in Garamond

Manufactured in the United States of America

1   3   5   7   9   10   8   6   4   2

Library of Congress Cataloging-in-Publication Data is available.

ISBN 0-7432-2888-X

For my mother, Barbara Ann Tully McBride,
in love and memory
&
for Edna O'Brien

ACKNOWLEDGMENTS

I am indebted to my editor, Doris Cooper, and to my agent, Regula Noetzli, for believing in me and in this book. Thanks also to Tracy Handley, Nancy Graham, Joan Howard, Ciaran O'Reilly, Brendan O'Reilly, and Doreen Schecter for the various ways they helped contribute to the life of this book.

Deep gratitude and love to my husband, Neil, for his patience and support. And to my daughter, Miranda, my light and my angel. Much love and thanks to Jane Lury for her guidance and compassion, and to Carolina Conroy, Irish Empress of Dresses.

Begin a voyage across the clear sea,
If you would reach the Land of Women.

—early Irish text (translated by Caitlin Matthews)

PART ONE

THE LAND OF MOTHERLESS GIRLS

siempre, siempre: jardín de mi agonía,
tu cuerpo fugitivo para siempre . . .

always, always: garden of my agony
your body elusive always . . .
—FEDERICO GARCÍA LORCA

ONE

When she closes her eyes, Fiona recalls the pale

smells of her mother's skin and hair; a smell like new

muslin washed in salt water and left to dry in the

wind. She tries to remember her mother's voice, and

the pitch and treble of it passes through her, the

rhythm of it so clear that for the shock of a moment

they are returned to one another in the way they had

been when she was small, connected by frail strings.

Displaced by the power of the memory, she sits

up in bed to prove to herself that she is in Santa Fe, in her house on Delgado Street, with the cottonwood tree outside her bedroom window, her father's boxes and papers cluttering the floor in hopeless disarray. The dry mountain air outside is black and still, full of cricket noise.

As she switches on the lamp, the sudden light hurts her eyes. In the dark she had remembered her mother's face clearly, but now it is all shifting, unresolved particles.

She gets up and goes outside onto the porch. The night air is cold, the sky vast and brilliant with stars over the cottonwoods and the stands of tamarisk trees. She can hear the rushing of the Santa Fe River, the heavy snows of the previous winter melting now, coming down from the Sangre de Cristo Mountains. Fiona sits on the porch chair and shivers. There is a storm ring around the moon, something she'd seen a few times in Ireland, but never before in New Mexico.

The light from her bedroom window illuminates her lap, and she gazes at the green and white pattern of leaves on her nightgown, seized by the memory of their old flat in Athlone, the faded green and white floral wallpaper, soft in places from the dampness. She remembers when she was seven years old and she and her mother, Jane, were about to leave that flat where Fiona had been born and go to Roundstone, where Jane was from, along the rocky Atlantic coast in the west of Ireland.

Fiona had been afraid to move to Roundstone. Jane had told her haunting stories of Presentation orphanage on the cliff, where she had grown up. The girls' mothers were buried in the graveyard with the white stone crosses that could be seen from the dormitory window. Mothers who had died giving birth to their daughters. Girls were buried there, too, the frailer ones who hadn't lasted.

"Sometimes we gazed out into the cold at the boreens looking to see the souls of the floating dead," Jane had whispered to her. When Jane talked liked this, Fiona perceived a deepened smell of mildew coming from above the headboard; she imagined that the words awakened some dormant presence in the room, causing the wallpaper to breathe. "We were in awe of them who had passed into the next world, certain they were movin' around weightless and restless, floating in circles like they didn't know what to do with themselves."

Fiona thought of the dead mothers staring up at the dormitory windows, keeping vigil, hoping to catch a glimpse of their beloved child. Or the dead girls seeking out their sisters, or just trying to pass the time by watching the living.

A girl had once been found in a bog near the orphanage, a girl who, they would learn, had been dead for centuries, wearing a little pointed hat, her knees bent into her chest. Jane and some of the other orphans had trespassed, desperately curious when they'd heard that something shocking had been dug up. Before the man whose farm bordered the bog chased them away, Jane saw the creature lying on her side on a little stretcher. Jane had told Fiona that a picture of the bog girl had been published in a magazine and that she had the clipping.

Long before there'd been any talk of going to the west of Ireland, Fiona had searched through Jane's papers and photographs and found the clipping. The bog girl's face, though black and shiny as polished stone, was clear. A wide, smooth forehead and a resigned expression. A bit of tension at one side of her mouth made her appear slightly irritated. She clutched what looked like a piece of rope in her two hands.

"Why is the girl so dark and shiny?" Fiona had asked.

"From centuries of soaking in the bog."

"Why is she holding that rope?"

"It isn't rope, Fiona."

"What is it?"

"A braid of hair."

"Is it her own hair?"

"They don't think so."

"Whose then?"

"It's a mystery," Jane had said.

Jane was taking them from Athlone in central Ireland, and directly west to that dangerous place, the heart of the bogs where mothers and daughters lost each other.

For as far back as Fiona could remember, Jane had complained that she hated Athlone. She had persuaded everyone at her seamstress job that she was married to Ronan Keane, Fiona's father, and that he came and went because it was the nature of his job.

Jane confided the truth to a woman she was friendly with, but when they had a row, the woman told everyone on the job. Jane came home mortified one day, one of the bookkeepers having called her a name she would not repeat. She never went back and set her mind on returning to Roundstone. It was the place she knew, where she'd been born, she said. She should never have left it. There was a certain beloved nun from the orphanage that she missed, she said. The French nun, Sister Delphine.

"The Irish are a small-minded people," Jane had chanted as she wept. She'd said it again and again, sitting on the bed, shaking her head. "The French understand human frailty."

She kept on her dresser a photograph of the old nun standing outside the convent in the sun, holding her veil to her head in a high wind.

The morning they were to leave, Fiona tried to lock herself into the bedroom. The creaking floor and the bed's curving iron headboard with the peeling white paint, even the musty wallpaper, had become for her a source of comfort. Jane managed to open the door. Fiona fought her, screaming and refusing to leave. The hysteria had gone on and on into the afternoon until Jane was furious and threatened to leave by herself. Fiona was still tremoring from the tears when they'd got on the bus.

When they'd been riding steadily for ten or fifteen minutes, Jane sighed and fell quiet. She'd looked to the window. Fiona knew from Jane's uneven breaths, her quiet swallowing, that she was holding back tears.

Letting go of the effort she'd been maintaining all day, Jane had pushed the seat partition up between them and drawn Fiona close. "Little love," she whispered. "The place will be familiar to you."

"Why?"

Jane had thought for a while and then said, "Because it's a part of both of us."

Fiona goes back inside and gets into bed. She wants to sleep, to let go of the memories. Before she turns off the light she struggles to root herself in the present, fixing her attention on the big oak dresser her father gave her and the objects she's placed on top of it, things that give her comfort. An antique silver brush and comb, a sandalwood box where she keeps her earrings. Her eyes settle on a small red bottle that she bought at a flea market, a bottle that catches the light and is unusually cold to the touch.

Sometime during the telephone call from her mother's husband, Ned McGinty, she'd picked up that little bottle and held it. She hears his voice again and wonders if the strained sound to it was due to the poor connection she had from Ireland, or his reticent emotion.

"A car accident . . . ," he'd said. "On the Galway road. The garda said that your mother died instantly. So she did not suffer."

He'd said that twice.

But not until an hour or so after she'd hung up did Fiona find herself wondering how he could be so certain of this, take it so much for granted. There could have been moments, even minutes, that Jane had suffered. Tears and a ferocious indignation rise within her.

Fiona stares at the red bottle, the lamplight igniting its dips and curves. They'd had the funeral that morning, he'd said, and Fiona had not reacted. She had not asked him why he hadn't called her. Had he thought she would not come? She does not even know the date of her mother's death. A wave of nausea moves through her.

She tells herself that in the morning she will telephone her mother's friend Noreen Feeney; that she will have a long conversation with her. She will find out the date of her mother's death.

She switches off the lamp, but each time she moves toward sleep, she hears a distant rush of ocean, a faint noise of gulls and breakers. She holds her breath and listens intently, and the sound stops.

But when she tries again to relax, the waves return, softly crashing, growing slowly to a roar.

From the outside, Presentation orphanage looked like a vast castle, set as it was on a rocky summit, the wind wild in the trees behind it. Inside, it was a maze of narrow hallways and dim, austere rooms. The nun, Sister Delphine, tall and willowy with frail, dry skin etched with many delicate little lines, light coming through her cheeks like rays through a paper lamp, swept toward them with her arms open.

"Little Jane. Dear little Jane," the nun sang in her French accent, the sound soft and guttural and sweet, embarrassing to Fiona.

"He still hasn't married me, Sister," Jane said, and dissolved into tears, the nun leading her to a hardwood bench, putting her arms around her. "Sssshhh. Sssshhh, little Jane O'Faolain."

Moved by Jane's emotion, hot tears had rolled down Fiona's face, her hands still folded in her lap, in the way her mother had shown her she must sit in the presence of the nun.

Jane looked feverish, shiny and pink of skin; the nun's continued incantation of her name worked a transformative magic on her, tears rinsing years away from her, reducing her to the very girl she'd once been. The girl Jane O'Faolain.

Unable to restrain herself, Fiona rose from her chair and knelt before her mother, joining the nun in chanting her mother's name. She touched the side of Jane's face and, smoothing her hair away from the dampness of her temples, ran her hand through the length of it again and again like a comb.

Sister Delphine told them that she had arranged for the house they would live in, a house that had belonged to a nun's cousin, a man now too old to keep up with the small bit of a farm that had been in his family for centuries.

"You should sew again, Jane," Sister Delphine said. "I think you'd do well. There's a demand."

Sister Delphine had saved one of Jane's notebooks, a green one, with a creased cover. The finger-worn pages crackled as Jane separated them. On every page were two or three drawings of dresses, some in soft, faded pencil, some in ink, all opulent in design: gowns with small, fitted waists and voluminous skirts. Some drawings had been erased over many times and redrawn.

"Such a romantic girl," Sister Delphine said affectionately, tilting her head as she looked at Jane, touching the hair at her temple.

"Sister Conception and Sister Elma often receive commissions for bridal gowns in the spring, but they're too old for it now. They turn girls away. We could direct girls to you. The dresses from the bridal shop in Galway are overmanufactured and overpriced."

Jane looked at her, full of consideration.

"And the orphans only make bone lace, nothing good enough for bridal veils."

"Sister Elma always said that these designs were meant for another century," Jane said.

"Not if you make them as wedding dresses," Sister Delphine said. "These are perfect for wedding dresses."

Jane led Fiona through halls tremulous with nuns' footsteps, echoes of girls' voices, watery and high-pitched. They arrived at the sewing room where Jane had learned the art of dressmaking. A heavyset nun on her knees attended the elaborate hems of a white dress on a headless figure. "Sister Elma," Jane said in a quiet, affectionate voice, and the nun looked up and nodded, smiling, lips clamped shut on three straight pins. Her damp eyes bulged.

At a table under a window, a group of girls labored with needles and thread. Fiona stared, captivated by the deft rhythms of their hands.

One of the lacemakers, a dark-haired girl older than Fiona, shot her an angry look, and Fiona wondered if that girl had a mother. Some girls who came to school here, she knew, lived with their families in Roundstone or nearby villages, and the rest were orphans. She wondered if Sister Delphine held each of the orphans at night, chanting their name the way she had with her mother, to remind them who they were.

Fiona was afraid to see what they were crafting, maybe the stuff called bone lace. She wondered with a shiver if there was something skeletal about it; if it was used to embellish the shrouds of dead people. It was the orphans, Sister Delphine had said, who manufactured this lace. Her mother had made it, and now Fiona wondered if it would be her lot to make it, too.

Jane opened a drawer full of fabrics and grazed her fingers over each one. "Silk . . . brocade . . . organza . . . pure Irish linen." Each word carried on her breath. She drew out a piece of silk and touched it to her cheek. Closing her eyes, she let out a little sound of pleasure. Then she offered it to Fiona, who did the same, and her heart floated with the sensation. It was soft and alive but cool, and when it brushed her skin, it made a whispering sound.

In the morning the telephone awakens Fiona. She lets the answering machine pick it up. It's the woman from the Armory for the Arts again who wants to organize a retrospective of Fiona's father's photographs. With poorly hidden irritation in her voice, the woman offers again to go through the material herself. Fiona's said no to her twice before, feeling protective of the boxes her father left to her. There are so many pictures she has not seen. Dense numbers of them, packed away in slides and frail, nearly opaque negatives. Yet, for almost two years now since his death, she's only skimmed the surface.

Fiona has to fight the sensation of being small and helpless against the woman's voice. She sits up in bed and stares at the boxes.

She sold her father's big house in Nambe after he died and bought this house in Santa Fe, hoping to open a little dress shop right in the front room. She'd decided that she'd make the dresses she'd sell, starting simple. She bought a hundred yards of gauzy Indian cottons and plain, light Irish linens. She designed an easy pattern, a summer dress she could once have cut, pinned, and seamed in her sleep.

But she has been unable to motivate herself to sew, the concentration that had once come so naturally to her now requiring tremendous effort.

Four or five times in the past year while browsing in the downtown stores, she had spotted garments with unusual designs or eccentrically fashioned sleeves. To find the shapes of the pieces so that she could make a pattern, she'd bought the garments, separating the seams carefully, filletting the stitchwork. But then she'd left the pieces on her shelves, never making the patterns or even attempting to reconstruct what she had dismembered. She wonders if somewhere in her mind she knew when she set out each time to the task that she would not follow through; that she found some perverse satisfaction in unraveling the careful work that had formed them.

Yet in her thoughts she sees her store open for business, a bright Santa Fe day, one of her dresses hanging from a hook on the front porch, undulating in the breeze.

This house is not that far off the beaten track. The tourists could find her easily, right off Canyon Road. She could advertise in the *Pasa Tiempo* and leave flyers at the La Fonda and the Inn at Loretto.

She bought a wicker chair with a large round back, imagining it would be a nice addition to the shop, but even before she'd received news of her mother's death, she'd found herself daydreaming in this chair, sinking into lethargy, unable to organize herself, to rise to the complications of such an undertaking.

She'd seen this house many years before when she and her father had driven past it on the way from a Canyon Road gallery. She remembered it because of its pitched roof and the towering red hollyhocks behind the black, wrought-iron Victorian fence, unusual on this particular old Santa Fe street where all the houses are surrounded by smooth, low adobe walls.

The first thing the Realtor had pointed out when Fiona'd come to look a year ago was the arched, leaded-glass window inset between splayed walls. The house had other interesting features, a mullioned door in the bedroom leading out onto the porch, various niches and alcoves, traditional spots to keep santos and bultos. But she'd kept going back to the window, the smoky glass giving a dimmer patina to the bright Santa Fe daylight, making it appear overcast. More like Irish light, she'd thought, faintly startled by the idea.

Standing in its penumbra, she'd begun to feel uneasy.

She thanked the Realtor for his time and left. But she'd thought for days about the house, and late one night she'd walked up Delgado Street and, after standing a while across the road, gone through the gate and to the door, which she found unlocked.

Inside, she went right to the window. Even at night she could not stop gazing at it. The many little panes reflected the room and her own shadow in various squares like dark mirror, each pane set at an almost indetectably different angle from the other. She sat in a shadow against the wall, facing the window, and experienced a sense of infinite safety. Sighing, she'd felt her muscles soften, the house emitting fortitude.

She goes into the kitchen and puts on the kettle for coffee. A few letters had come from Jane over the past twelve years since she's seen her, but Fiona never answered any of them. She thinks about Noreen Feeney, but in the bright of morning the thought of calling her does not offer the reassurance it did the night before. She has to fight an urge to sink into the wicker chair. She needs to leave the house, she tells herself. To set herself to a task.

She wants to buy a mirror, something that would make a nice addition to the shop. Something old-fashioned, maybe Victorian to keep with the mood set by the wrought-iron fence. She was in a shop once in Durango, or in Mesa Verde, filled with hanging ferns, furnished with antiqued white shelves and display tables.

A few months back she had read in the Sunday *New Mexican*

that the Aragon family had expanded their antique-restoration business; that they'd bought a gutted church near Santuario in Chimayo. She imagines that they have a mirror.

After she finishes her coffee, she showers and puts on her faded jeans and a loose, white cotton blouse and drives along the Paseo de Peralta and out onto the Espanola highway. It is almost noon and she smells rain coming. Low winds runnel through the widening patches of mesa on the roadside leading out of town.

When she reaches Tesuque, lightning makes nervous lanterns of the clouds. By the time she's driven up the rocky earth roads to Aragon's, a front of shadow has moved into the sky. When she gets out of the car, a raw wind exhilarates her.

There are still large, white holy-water fonts in the vestibule of Aragon's Antiques and Restoration, and a broken fresco of La Trinidad, the triplet Christs sitting together, the two on the outside pointing at the thorny, inflamed heart of the one in the center. The vast main room is dim and cool, whitewashed plastered adobe. Dark vigas at the high cathedral ceilings.

The first room houses delicate pieces: opulently carved tables, upholstered chairs in velvets and rose brocades, Victorian-looking statues and tiresome bric-a-brac. Behind a reception desk, a young woman glances up at Fiona expressionlessly. Fiona nods but the woman does not acknowledge her, looking back down at her ledger. Fiona walks unobtrusively past her and into the next room, where she enters a forest of archaic dressers and breakfronts and chiffoniers. The passageways become increasingly narrow as she goes, tall wardrobes casting shade into the lanes beneath them. She stops and opens a small drawer, and it exhales a dusty, rosy-smelling draft. She opens more drawers distractedly, breathing and smelling. She forgets herself, taking in the coolness the furniture exudes around her like a system of living trees. She runs a finger over the antlers of a deer carved in decorative relief on the side of a balustrade.

When she comes into a clearing, she sits down on a wooden bench, studying the peculiar masts and turrets rising from an arbor of Gothic-looking cabinets.

"Please don't sit on the bench."

Fiona gasps and turns. The woman from the reception desk is standing in an interval between furniture. Fiona gets to her feet.

"I didn't mean to scare you," the woman says. She has short, black hair and eyebrows enhanced by black pencil.

"It's all right."

The woman's eyes glow mistrustfully. "That bench needs work. My husband and his brother brought it back from a demolished church in Spain."

"Oh, I'm sorry."

"Are you looking for something in particular?"

"I'm looking for a mirror to fill a wall."

"To *fill* it?"

"Well, it's for my shop in Santa Fe. I have a shop and I need a mirror."

"What kind of shop?"

"A dress shop."

"Oh." Fiona thinks she sees the shadow of a smirk on the woman's face. "There are no mirrors in this room, except the ones attached to furniture. Go downstairs and look. There are a few."

"Thanks." Fiona follows the woman back through the lane and out of the forest. The woman points at the staircase and returns to her desk as Fiona descends.

*

One mirror downstairs captures her attention, but it is nothing dainty or Victorian like the one she's had in mind. The frame is heavy and dark, minutely carved, the crevices dusted in gold leaf. As she stares at herself, her face softly distorted by a ripple on its surface, she hears a man cough from some nearby room. She sees a bright, unnatural light issuing through the crack of an open door.

Fiona looks into the vast, cool basement room. On a table, with a single lamp bright as a stage light shining down on it, stands the partially fractured terra-cotta figure of a girl, an urchin or ragamuffin about three feet tall, wearing a feverish expression on her cracked, stained face.

A man leans in close to it with a small brush, gingerly applying something to one of the figure's hands, which is caught in a graceful gesture a few inches from its heart.

Fiona is intrigued by the face, unable to distinguish whether it is joy or suffering she sees in the expression. She wonders if it is a saint. The stains that run down from the figure's eyes suggest tears, but her aqua green dress runs with the same dark trickles.

Fiona leans into the doorway, her attention held by the patience with which the man applies the brush. With his other hand he holds the chin of the saint between his thumb and forefinger. He scrutinizes her face so intently and gets so close to it that Fiona imagines he is going to kiss it.

The man's grace and delicate sensibility are at odds with his largeness. He is big, wide-shouldered. A long vein ripples around one forearm and runs up, disappearing under the cap sleeve of his black T-shirt.

Each smooth, unbroken motion of his brush suggests devotion. He seems to be tracing the ancient workmanship, memorizing it.

He reaches over to his table of little colored bottles and opens one. A sharp smell of herbs escapes and rushes Fiona, dragging after it a fume of alcohol. He dabs the girl's fingers with the solution.

His hair is caught in a negligent ponytail, held by a coarse string of leather. He is sweating and a few loose black strands of hair glisten when they catch the light. A few cling to the dampness at his temples.

The man applies his brush again and Fiona finds herself entranced by its soft repetitions. She recognizes the pleasure he derives from such concentrated labor. She remembers the way the daylight had changed across the dressmaker's table, how a morning could become an afternoon, cutting and pinning fabric, and afternoon turn into evening with the pieces of a dress basted on a dressform. With diligence and focus, something could become beautiful and take form.

Over the last minutes the line of sweat along the man's backbone has deepened on his shirt. She has almost forgotten the woman upstairs, and now, hearing the soft booms of footsteps descending the stairs, wonders if this man she's been watching is the woman's husband.

But it's not a woman's voice that speaks to her from behind. "Are you interested in restorations?"

She turns suddenly.

"I'm Joe Aragon," a man says, holding his hand out proudly to her. His jaw slides a little as he smiles.

She shakes his hand. "Is that the figure of a saint?" She

looks back in and notices that the other man is looking at her for the first time.

This proud one, Joe Aragon, standing with her in the bright room of mirrors, is as tall as the other but thinner. His hair is shorter, too, and overgroomed, Fiona thinks. She can see where the teeth of a comb last ran through it.

His eyes travel down her neck and survey the skin of her chest. She becomes self-conscious of her redheaded, freckled complexion; something she's never grown easy with living in New Mexico. A lot of Hispanic men like this one give her lustful, incredulous looks. She is a curiosity to them.

"My brother, Carlos," he begins, pointing at the man restoring the figure, "thought it was La Alma de Maria. The Soul of the Virgin. He says he saw a Spanish Virgin like her once, wearing green. But now, he thinks she has a relation to a lost ship of the Spanish Armada."

"What kind of relation?"

"Some of the Spaniards made statues and figures in honor of the ships that were wrecked."

"Along the western coast of Ireland," Fiona adds.

His eyes open a bit wider and she senses his surprise. "Yes," he says, and smiles at her, revealing prominent, slightly buck teeth, his upper lip rising and curling at one corner. He is watching her closely now, and she feels the heat of a flush go up in her face.

"José," the woman calls from the summit of the stairs.

He rolls his eyes and turns to face her. The woman lets loose a soft tirade in Spanish, and he climbs the stairs to meet it.

Fiona does not look in again at Carlos Aragon. Her eyes rake the room for mirrors, and she catches her own face looking back at her in the one with the ripple on its surface. She blames her startled expression on hearing lore familiar to her from her girlhood, as if her Irish past is pursuing her, finding her in the unlikeliest places.

José and his wife are arguing in the forest of furniture, and Fiona is able to slip out unobtrusively, laughing to herself when she hears the wife call him a *cavronne*.

The wind is high when she walks outside, dry earth stinging her face, hitting the window of her car as she gets in, slams the door, and starts the engine. Driving back into Santa Fe, she watches the tumbleweeds on the mesa, the wind rattling the windows of her old car.

TWO

Three ships of the Spanish Armada had been wrecked in the jagged rocks on the beach near Roundstone.

Fiona looks at the photographs her father took of her mother on that precipitous stretch of sand behind Presentation orphanage. It's been years since she's looked at these. Her father had kept them arranged, she knows, in the order he had taken them.

The first one shows sixteen-year-old Jane tilting

her head and smiling coyly, one strand of hair whipping up into the air. Fiona finds it difficult to focus long on her mother's girlish face, which fills her with a tender, woeful impression, though this first picture Fiona had seen almost every day of her early life. Jane had kept a copy of it framed and hanging in the kitchen in Roundstone near the shrine to the Virgin. Candles had often been lit before it.

Its proximity to the stove had caused its edges to curl and discolor slightly. The glass of the frame grew cloudy, so Jane took it down periodically to clean it. Fiona remembers Jane gazing into the soft face that had once been her own, drawing at her cigarette until its glow was reflected on the glass that encased it.

But now so many years having passed, what strikes Fiona is that she cannot isolate the landscape from Jane, though she can see that her father had seen it only as backdrop. She cannot separate the face of this girl from the peculiar light and the wind and the graveyard cross; the bit of gate and gable from the gloomy convent above on the cliff. He had not known how inextricably these landmarks were part of Jane.

Perhaps, Fiona thinks, it was the fatefulness of that particular day that so infused the light, creamy and permeable in places, dark and pewtery in others, atmospheric as a holy picture. This was the day her parents had first met. And the day Fiona was conceived.

In the second photograph, Jane is running away from the sea, which rises in aggressive peaks, chasing her, her legs and hair a blur of motion. In the third, Jane runs toward the camera, a stillness in her face, a contemplativeness at odds with the apparent motion of her body. The clouds look as textured as raveled cloth, their edges ignited.

*

When Fiona was seven, she came with Jane to this beach. The sea had appealed to Fiona immediately. The incoming booms of the surf sent thrills up her spine. It *was* unexplainably familiar to her, though the smell of it made her mysteriously sad.

That first day they'd gone to the beach together, they'd climbed down from the point. Jane took off her shoes, threw them into the dune grass, and ran out after the tide. When it turned, she ran inland laughing wildly as it overtook her, soaking her skirt.

Fiona took off her shoes, weighting them with sand, and approached the tide with cautious excitement. When it touched her feet, she squealed with the cold. They made a game of it, her mother always the bolder one, holding her skirt up around her waist, falling deliriously a few times to her knees, the surf rushing her. They ran up the beach picking up shells, throwing them out again into the surf, chasing the tide and running from it.

The pictures fill Fiona with the old pain of Jane's yearning for Ronan.

There'd been a thousand charms she had assisted Jane with. Charms to summon the beloved. Throwing snippets of hair and fingernail clippings into the fire while calling out his name, sprinkling salt on the four corners of Jane's bed. Capturing Jane's tears in a tiny glass bottle for various purposes: to rub into his name written in red ink on cloth, to anoint objects that he'd once touched. Jane hung an old nightgown she'd worn when she'd slept with Ronan on the curtain rod, where it presided over them all night. They made a tiny braid out of two strands of Jane's hair and one strand of Fiona's and buried it in the mud near the river that was hidden in trees.

Once they'd taken the nightgown to the river, where Jane

washed it in the water, her eyes flitting up constantly to the opposite bank. Fiona had so possessed herself with Jane's desire that she'd gone into a swoon, trembling and pointing, imagining she saw Ronan's reflection in the water.

Looking at the photographs now, she poses the same question to the air as Jane had posed many times in the past: How could Ronan Keane have captured such nuance in Jane and not have loved her? Maybe he loved her that day, Fiona says to herself. Maybe he managed to love her every now and then, the times he'd been with her in the years to follow that day.

It comes to her as if out of the air. The moment before, the memory was not there, and now it is, as if it has never been lost. They'd been in Roundstone for a week, staying with the nuns, when Jane up and left Fiona there alone in the orphanage. For how long? she wonders. A few days? A fortnight? She isn't certain, but her heart starts up at a tremendous rate.

In the sewing room Jane told Fiona that she was going to Dublin to see Ronan. Fiona remembers the saline vapors of the sea coming in the screens and a smell of faintly charred cloth that was the work of the old nun's iron pressing fabric, gargling hoarsely with its throatful of steam each time it was set upright.

Jane had squeezed Fiona's hand, avoiding her eyes. Patches of color were high on Jane's cheeks. Fiona sensed her anticipation. It was always that way. Jane was ashamed of the way things stood with Ronan Keane, but there was some willingness in her, some excitement that kept her to him. He'd contacted her, Jane said. He wanted to see her. Fiona would stay with the nuns. It would only be a few days, she said.

For a moment after she'd said this, Fiona had not breathed. But when Jane stood, the room began to spin. Fiona could not see. She grabbed her mother's skirt, and a struggle ensued.

"Only a few days," Jane cried, anger in her voice at Fiona's wildness. Fiona kicked her and held to her ankles, Jane dragging her toward the door. Fiona would hold her there. She would not let her disappear.

Two nuns came and one of them extricated her from Jane.

"Animal!" Jane had cried. "You're acting like an animal!"

How many days had Fiona been alone in Presentation orphanage? That was her first profound loss of Jane. And now with the news of Jane's death, Fiona is plummeted in a similar way, all the old rage rising up in her, all the ancient anguish.

In the morning, resolved to telephone Noreen Feeney, Fiona rifles through her old papers where she knows she has a small address book with Roundstone phone numbers in it. She is stunned to come upon the magazine clipping of the bog girl. She'd been so fascinated by it as a child that Jane had given it to her. But like all things overly familiar, it had grown invisible to her. A folded piece of paper among her photographs and letters. Faded newspaper, yellowed now with time. She had remembered the girl's face as resigned, but now she sees a blightedness in the expression, a tightness in the jaw. She puts it away, too flustered now to telephone Noreen.

She leaves the house and drives around the Paseo, north along St. Francis Drive toward Española, finding relief in the breadth and height of the land, the mesas running along into infinite distance, the range of the Jemez Mountains to the west, the more familiar Sangre de Cristos to the east. The landscape is dry, half-barren. She sees the bog girl in her mind and steps hard on the gas, unable to reconcile herself with the desperate way the child clings to the braid of hair, the way her knees fold in close to her chest. Such a creature could not be unearthed here in New Mexico, she tells herself. The dead can dry and go to dust and not be revealed in centuries to come in their postures of suffering and shame.

Seeing the tight little jaw, Fiona knows suddenly that the girl had died angry. She pulls the car to the side of the highway and closes her eyes. She can smell the bog, wet briers. A bonfire. She presses her forehead to the steering wheel.

It seems a long time she remains here. Each car that zooms past makes a mournful noise in the distance. Even with her eyes closed, Fiona feels the light changing. In the mesa, just beyond where she is parked, wind begins to seethe in a group of juniper trees. When she looks into the sky, the clouds have closed and blackened. The shower comes quick and hard. She thinks of the man Carlos at Aragon's Antiques and Restoration, calmly ministering to the battered figure. Fiona suddenly craves the cool and silence of that underground room where she imagines Carlos Aragon still stands, methodically applying his balms and his oils.

She starts the car again and heads for Santuario.

A dark green pickup truck is parked in front of Aragon's, and she knows somehow that it belongs to Carlos.

The massive, dry wood door swings on its iron hinge with a gentle push. She goes inside, moving through the dim rooms. A carved ebony figure of a woman on a mantel regards her as she passes. She had not noticed it there before, and it feels now like a replacement for José Aragon's vigilant wife. She sees the light behind the half-open door as she descends the stairs.

Now, peering quietly in, she sees the figure of the girl, alone and floodlit, her elated face cleansed pure. The tones of her flesh are restored and polished; it looks as if she is sweating. Her eyes brim with the same brilliance as her skin.

Drawn to her, Fiona walks in for a closer look and sees a design of Celtic knots etched on the bodice of the girl's dress. She smells cigarette smoke and looks into the shadows. Carlos Aragon is sitting in a chair with his legs crossed. She stops and doesn't move, her eyes on him.

"I saw you working on her yesterday," Fiona says, hoping this will justify her trespassing.

But the silence that follows is uncomfortable. After a beat he says, "My sister-in-law isn't here today. Is there something upstairs you're interested in?"

"No," she answers softly. "No."

She is retreating from the room, almost at the door, when his voice wafts out from the shadows after her. "There are salt crystals in the statue's hair."

She turns. "Salt crystals?"

"In the crevices of her hair. Tiny salt crystals." The ash glows as he takes a drag of his cigarette. Maybe, Fiona thinks, it's the reverence with which she approached the figure that's made him decide to share this with her. The smoke from his exhalation reaches her where she stands. She watches it ripple up around the figure's head.

"Your brother told me that you found her in Spain."

"Yes, near La Coruña on the sea."

"Is that the Mediterranean Sea?"

"No. It's the Atlantic, the far north of Spain."

"She has Celtic knots on her dress . . ."

"Yes," he says. "Northern Spain, Galicia, is Celtic."

He puts the cigarette out in an ashtray at his feet, then stands and joins her in the floodlights. "I have to deal with the crystals. I'm not sure if they'll cause decomposition or not. And after that, I have to apply another sealing solution. I've brought her here and now I have to keep her from turning to dust."

A single dimple appears in one cheek when he smiles.

He picks up a magnifying glass and leans into the statue, focused on a carved curl of hair. In the bright light Fiona studies the bone structure of his face. She thinks of the strong stone heads of Constantinople. There's something arcane about him, and dark. His skin is moist and even as fine brown silk.

He gives her the magnifying glass: "Look."

She takes it and peers through. The crystals are delicate as hairs, but faceted, leaning at odd angles like ghostly demolished buildings. She glances at him and sees that he is looking at her arm, wondering, she thinks, over the frailty and composition of her skin, densely freckled and fraught with fine golden-red hair, but with a sudden pink belly, like the under furl of a conch shell. She wonders if he can read the history printed on her skin; skin that cannot make peace with sun and dry air.

When she looks at him again, he is studying her face. She holds his eyes and imagines that at any moment he will take her chin between his thumb and forefinger, the way she'd seen him do with the statue, and bring his face close to hers. A flare of heat for him licks the inside of her chest and rushes down in a flurry between her legs.

She imagines offering herself to his care; letting him paint her in cool unguents.

The noise of rain spatters the window at the top of the room that is level with the earth, and the sound of it breaks some spell for her. She averts her eyes from his, and she is afraid to look at him again; afraid that her own face will look as beseeching, as crazed, as the face of the little urchin saint.

"My name is Carlos."

"I'm Fiona." She's still looking past him into the gloom.

She turns back to the figure, searching it. After a moment of silence, he says, "I'm finished here."

She nods and moves toward the door.

He switches off the floodlight, leaving the figure in darkness. He locks the basement door and they move up the dim stairs and through the passages of furniture.

When he opens the massive wooden door, the rain has deepened to a downpour.

"You can wait here a bit if you like," he says, gesturing to the bench. "I'm going to."

They sit together, the door wide open, and look out at the rain. This old church is close to the river, and the land around it is verdant, full of trees. The air is rich with the green smell of the pink broom tamarisks and the river trees.

The silence between them is uncomfortable. "Irish air," Fiona says, remembering his interest in the Armada.

"Irish?" he asks. With her peripheral vision she sees him focused on her.

"Yes."

"I thought you might be from Ireland."

"I moved here when I was eighteen."

"What's your last name?"

She pauses. Even now at the age of thirty, the question causes her heart to speed up.

"My father was Ronan Keane."

His eyes widen. "Really?" The Aragons owned one of the galleries where her father once exhibited his photographs. "I heard of his death. I'm sorry."

She nods.

"Last year, wasn't it?" he asks.

"Almost two years ago."

There'd been an article in *The New Mexican* about Ronan at the time, a big spread with some of his photographs. His death had been sudden. For a week he'd had headaches, and then one morning he didn't wake up. The doctor was certain it had been a blood clot in the brain.

"I'm sorry," he says again.

The silence is strained. The rain intensifies and slows, then intensifies again.

"Irish air," he says. She meets his eyes and sees in them again that same curiosity.

"It's like the sea air . . . has crossed a continent to find me," she hears herself say. She feels faintly self-conscious, so she smiles at him as if there is humor in what she's said. But the words touch the sadness at the edge of her and she wishes she had not said them.

"I love Ireland," he says, a new animation in his voice.

She nods.

"You might say even that I'm a little obsessed with Ireland."

She looks away from him. People have all kinds of odd notions about Ireland. She is afraid he will disappoint her by being one of them.

"Your brother told me that you think the figure might represent a monument to one of the Armada ships."

"Yes," he says, leaning toward her slightly.

"Why are you so interested in the Armada ships?"

"An ancestor of mine was on one of the ships that was wrecked on the western coast of Ireland."

"So you search for Spanish relics in the sea?"

"Yes, you could say that," he says, smiling. It occurs to her that she might tell him that she grew up on a beach known for its lore about Spanish shipwrecks. She is about to ask him where his ancestor's ship went down when he asks suddenly, "Why did you leave Ireland?"

The question silences her. She shakes her head slightly and tries to think of something to say, but a heaviness overcomes her. The rain has almost stopped and she stands up.

For a few moments she doesn't move but continues to gaze out into the rain. She feels his expectation on the air. There is something palpable and sympathetic between them that she cannot articulate.

The expression on his face when she turns to look at him is at once grave and curious.

"Thank you for letting me look at the statue," she says.

He gives her half a smile, and she goes through the light rain to her car.

Before she gets the wipers started, she sees him through the drizzling windshield moving toward his truck.

She drives through the wet night into Santa Fe and wonders if the headlights on a truck behind her are his.

She turns onto the Paseo, but the truck does not follow.

Carlos Aragon has stirred her physically. She thinks of Michael Devlin, of what they did secretly together in the barley field that would grow lavish and dense and fantastically tall, a kind of woodland in which she might have gotten lost. But the past is like terrain, and she must journey from one place to get to the next.

THREE

The world stopped when Jane went to Dublin. Sister Delphine's warbling had only intensified Fiona's anguish. She cried at night keeping the nuns awake, so they moved her to the dormitory with the orphans where the girls stared and whispered about her.

A girl with a soft voice, whom she did not open her eyes to look at, told her not to be sad, because sad children attract ghosts. Fiona was delirious, her senses deranged with anticipation, startling awake, hallucinating her mother, feeling the cold of her fingers and the heat of her breath. And each time she realized that her mother was not really there, devastation overtook her.

In the morning she was instructed to stay with the lace-maker orphans, following them, wan and exhausted, through dim gray-green corridors. While they worked irritably under the light of the window, Fiona passed pins to Sister Elma, who was setting the hem of a dress. The wide tulle skirt smelled of mothballs and hissed fussily at the nun as she brushed against it. The heavy silk of the bodice seemed mismatched with the weightlessness of the skirts. The old nun moved around the dressform like an attendant insect around an opulent queen.

When Sister Elma left the room, the tall girl, Julie, the girl who had looked crossly at Fiona that first day they were there, swore in a soft, easy voice, the same voice she might have used to pray, "Bloody, fat, old bitch of a nun," causing laughter from some girls, and glances of disapproval from others. Fiona wanted to join them, not knowing if she would be on the side of the amused or the disapproving. She was still nervous of the stuff called bone lace, afraid that if she got too close to it she was inviting grief. She sensed, too, that the orphans hated her because she had a mother. But her mother, Jane, was one of *them*. This truth moved under the surface of everything since she'd come here, stunning Fiona each time it appeared. All Jane knew of her own mother was that she had been a "slip of a girl" who had died not long after Jane arrived.

But Jane had never complained of that. It was husbandless-ness that plagued her, that made her anxious. And now Fiona was helping make a dress for some woman who would marry.

A wedding was, to Fiona, a kind of coronation. She imag-ined women in their gowns, standing on clouds like the Virgin, the winds gloriously working the skirts like sails. Women were entitled to this when they loved a man. But Jane had had no such ceremony. Fiona wondered if this had something to do with the fact that she'd had no mother. The right to marry seemed a kind of blood legacy you were either born with or not.

From her union with Ronan Keane, Jane had not acquired a coronation gown, but a daughter. A half orphan, a smaller, slightly distorted replica of herself.

Fiona thought about the last charm she and Jane had made to summon Ronan: the plait of hair, two strands of Jane's braided with one strand of her own. When they'd buried it in the mud near the river in Athlone, they had both wished intensely for Ronan, Jane having been sad over the gossiping women at work. If he'd come, perhaps they wouldn't leave Athlone. Fiona had been tense with anticipation. She'd walked through her days and nights ready for an epiphany. She'd imagined Ronan appearing suddenly, transcending distance, composing himself out of smoke and evaporation, salt and currents of river water.

The real man, the flesh-and-blood one who made the rare appearance, seemed crude in comparison with the one who might appear in response to unmitigated desire. The flesh-and-blood man was too quiet, too separate. He was difficult to read and awkward with Fiona. She secretly wanted the other one, a wise, gentle one who would nod his head at every urgent plea and utterance from either of their mouths. The one who would make everything all right and rescue Fiona from the Presentation orphanage.

Fiona crouched behind the dress where the girls could not see her, pretending to adjust the pins inserted into the hems. She reached up and touched the sluggish silk of the bodice, which held the cold like porcelain. This close it smelled sweet like treacle. As she sat back down, the net brushed at her hair, causing sparks of static.

She gazed at the dress in its stillness. It seemed asleep, only faintly stirring. She hated it. Nothing seemed to drive it. She wanted to take the scissors to it, make clean cuts at it.

At night, Fiona could see Julie's silhouette as she sat upright in her cot.

"Come with me," she ordered, and Fiona obeyed, drawn to Julie's troubling authority and excited by the illicit danger of moving at night through the dark, complex maze of halls. It occurred to Fiona that one of the hallways might end suddenly, doorless and overlooking the sea. She imagined this girl pushing her out. She saw herself hurtling though air and down into water, sinking to the bottom. When Jane returned, she'd suffer a terrible regret over having left Fiona.

They stopped in an icy corridor with rattling windows, and Julie sat down on the floor and lit a cigarette. It was Miss Dunleavy, one of the women who came to help the nuns, whose cardigan she'd taken it from. In the little bit of moonlight through the window, Fiona could see Julie studying her face, looking at her from under her eyebrows, the orange light deepening in her eyes each time she drew at the cigarette. The smoke she exhaled ascended, shifting and hanging in the faint light above them.

Fiona wanted something from the girl but was not sure what. She breathed the bitter smoke and her eyes ached.

"She'll not come back, you know," Julie said. "When they leave you here, it's a rare thing if they come back."

"She just went to Dublin to see my father. We're going to move into a house when she gets back."

"I know . . . the blue house on the other hill. Near the bog where they found the dead girl."

"Near that bog?"

"You know about the bog girl?" Julie asked.

"Yes, the one holding the bit of rope."

"Not rope. Hair. A braid of hair from her own mother's head."

"From her mother's head?"

"Yes."

"Was the mother found in the bog as well?"

"No. The braid had been cleanly cut, given to the girl as some pagan parting gift."

Julie was being cruel, but it did not matter. Fiona understood suddenly what she had wanted from her. There was a strange relief in hearing the worst possible thing, as if the anticipation she'd been keeping was too painful to hold on to any longer.

Julie seemed irritated that she could not make Fiona angry. She took the last draw of her cigarette, blew out the smoke, and then slowly extinguished it by stubbing it again and again on the cold tile.

"You know," Julie said indifferently, "your father is probably fucking the bejesus out of her at this very minute."

Fiona knew she was talking about the wrestling they did together in bed.

"You know what I'm talking about. She's having the bejesus fucked out of her and having a grand old time of it. Not a thought for you."

"My father's going to marry my mother," Fiona said, at a loss for words.

"Hah!"

Fiona followed Julie back through the hallway, repeating her claim that her father would marry her mother.

"Be bloody quiet," Julie said under her breath, "or I'll have to knuckle-punch you."

Back in bed, Fiona fell into a heavy, dreamless sleep.

In the morning when Fiona awakened, Jane was there, still wearing her coat, her cheeks cold with the morning air.

Fiona did not lift her head from the pillow but stared at her. It was even worse now than it had been before, the anger so wild and strong in her.

She did not speak to Jane but followed her instructions, going through the motions of leaving, the edges of her ears and the inside of her chest burning.

The blue, color-washed house was less than a mile away. Mr. Ryan, the hired man, drove them through an entrance gate at the bottom of the hill and up past the two small fields in front. At the back of the house the land descended into a valley, a patch of dark, fecund earth, the furrowed bog. The sky was sunless, olive-colored. Magpies careened and bickered, disappearing into the trees.

Inside there was a battered, musty sofa and a long, scrub-board table with four kitchen chairs. Wooden draining boards flanked the sink in the kitchen, which was an extension of the main room.

They would share a bedroom, not like in Athlone where Fiona had had her own small room. If Ronan Keane came, she might hear the chaotic breathing between them at night. A wave of nausea moved through her at the thought.

The hired man helped Jane unload the sewing things and

the dressforms that Sister Delphine had given her and went out again.

"You would have left me there if my father hadn't been tired of fucking the bejesus out of you."

Jane's lips trembled. She stood up and raised a hand as if she would slap Fiona but stopped herself and turned away from her.

The rage drained out of her and she stood looking down at the floor, her shoulders sloping as if her body were a terrible weight to her.

Mr. Ryan came back in the door and handed Jane a bucket of turf.

"From the bog outback?" Jane asked.

"The same bog they've always cut from," he said, his eyes slowly filling with a smile.

When he left, Fiona asked her, "Are you afraid the child might have left a finger or toe behind in the peat?"

"No," Jane said, made defensive by Fiona's tone. "I'm sure the turf never touched the girl herself." Jane looked at Fiona, appealing to her with wide, guilty eyes. The fury started up stronger in Fiona. She tightened her lips and wanted somehow to hurt her.

Seeing that, Jane turned back to the turf and sighed. She lit a match, the flame licking at a dark block, snapping and hesitating before encasing it, seamless as silk.

"It's blue, is it not?" Jane whispered. "Flame on turf this fresh?"

Fiona shivered, nervous of the aromatic warmth.

Four

Fiona telephones a lawyer, Mr. Vigil, whose name she finds in the yellow pages. She wants to make an appointment. There are questions she has regarding the form she is filling out for a resale license.

"You see, I don't have any employees now, but I may have a seamstress eventually if things go well."

He talks vaguely about withholding taxes and social security, then says, "If you have an accountant, he should also come to the appointment."

"I don't."

He pauses, then says, "Uh-huh."

He asks where her house is located, and when she tells him, he says that there should be no legal problem opening a shop in that area.

They set a time to meet, and just before he hangs up, she asks him to check on the town rules about the size of the sign she is allowed to put up.

He lets out a little laugh. "These are minor things."

She cannot tell if he is being reassuring or condescending.

When she hangs up, she wishes she hadn't called. Every time she's taken a practical step toward realizing the shop, she's become filled with doubts.

That evening, just past nine, Fiona leaves her house and walks north on Delgado in the streetlights to Acequia Madre, where the roots of ancient cottonwoods erupt from the sidewalks, their leaves and branches forming an arch over the narrow, winding road. A car passes slowly through like a lighted boat.

It is the end of April; temperately cool breezes cross the air like trade winds. She walks along Canyon Road, the adobe faces of dark galleries and shops perilously close to the road.

She smells piñon smoke and hears voices and sees lights on the patio at the Café de las Palomas Oscuras, which must only recently have opened its outside restaurant for the season.

As she passes on the other side of the street, she hears her name called out. Carlos Aragon stands near the table where he is finishing a meal with his brother, José, and his wife.

Fiona stops where she is, gazing at him, taken aback.

"Fiona," he calls to her, and gestures her over. The leaves of a giant cottonwood tree, reaching over the restaurant, rush exultant, then shift their direction again suddenly.

She crosses the street and goes in through the gate as Carlos pulls a chair away from an empty table and places it next to his.

José Aragon's wife is eyeing her, leaning against her husband's arm. "You know Della?" Carlos asks. Fiona nods to her and she nods back. "And José, of course," Carlos adds.

"Yes," Fiona says. José avoids Fiona's eyes, looking absently at the leaves of the cottonwood, which are rioting again in the lamplight.

"Would you like a glass of wine?" Carlos asks.

"Yes, thank you."

"Red?"

"Yes."

Carlos calls the waiter over and orders a bottle of Sangre de Toro. He is more forthcoming in his manner tonight, and Fiona wonders if it is the wine or the company of his familiars that influences him. She has the sense that he is excited to see her; perhaps he's been thinking about her.

"Fiona is from Ireland," he tells the others.

"Oh, well, that explains how you knew so quickly about the Spanish Armada," José says.

"I lived near a beach where it was said that three of the Armada ships were wrecked," Fiona says.

Carlos's eyes open wide. "Where?" he asks.

"Roundstone. County Galway."

"And one of those ships has recently been found!" Carlos says. "This is a very exciting time for people interested in the Armada wrecks. So many have been excavated in recent years. What was once only lore is now proven to be true!"

José and Della exchange a glance and Fiona looks curiously at them.

"José is sick of my obsession with the Armada," Carlos says.

José shrugs. "A terrible defeat for Spain."

"José is a conqueror," Carlos says, smiling. "He's happy here in Santa Fe where even the shopping centers, Coronado Center, De Vargas Plaza, are named after conquistadors."

José smiles wryly, his wife watching his face. She is sensual-looking in the candlelight, though her mistrustfulness makes her hard. She is like his watchdog and he is afraid of her. Fiona wonders what it is that holds them to each other.

"Yes, Spain is everywhere to be seen in Santa Fe," Fiona ventures. "And all the streets have beautiful Spanish names. Camino del Monte Sol. Calle de Sueños."

"Do you know that northern Spain looks very much like Ireland?" Carlos asks her.

"Really? I'm ashamed to say I never even knew that Galicia was Celtic until you told me."

"Yes, there are a lot of old connections. The Spanish have had a great affection for the Irish for many centuries."

"It was opportunistic, on both sides," José says. "They each needed more force against the English."

"There was more to it than that," Carlos says.

"Spain's entanglements with the Irish were ill-advised," José says. "Think of the Irish sheriffs who put Spanish survivors to death."

"That was under duress from the English," Carlos says, and looks at Fiona as if for affirmation, but both sides of the argument seem too simple.

José shakes his head. "You idealize the Irish, Carlos. Every collaboration between Spain and Ireland turned out disastrously."

Fiona's heart hammers in her chest.

Della smirks and looks imperious. With only a sip gone from her espresso cup, she says they ought to go, and José immediately stands.

"Good-bye," Della says, sternly polite, leaving the pink imprint of her lower lip on the small white cup. José leaves half a Dos Equis.

When they are gone, Carlos smiles at her.

"How is the figure? The girl in green?" she asks.

"I'm excited. I have a friend from Marseille, Gaston, who's pored over all the fading Armada documents in the European archives, and he thinks he has pieced together the story of my ancestor's ship. He's found evidence that the girl in green may actually be a monument made for the ship by friends and family of the men who were on it.

"The ship was called *La Alma Verde,* though when it was wrecked it may have been mistakenly documented under another name, because we cannot find any records. Even if a ship was lost sight of and not accounted for, there would be mention of it in the records. Where it was last seen or something."

"Do you have any idea where it may have been wrecked?"

"Gaston suspects in the Blasket Sound. We did a dive there a year and a half ago. For a few days I walked around thinking I had relics from my ancestor's ship. But it turned out the ship we'd found was called the *Maria Christina.*"

"How did you come upon the story?"

"It's been passed down in my family that we had an ancestor who survived an Armada wreck. But when I went to Betazos, the village he moved to when he returned to Spain after the wreck, I learned a much more detailed story." He pauses and she senses his excitement. "In the archives of that town, there's an actual document, enscribed in the seventeenth century, a copy of my ancestor's diary. I translated it."

"Your ancestor's diary?"

"Unlike most of the shipwrecked he survived and managed to escape torture and imprisonment by the English." He looks intently at Fiona and she feels again that curious bond of sympathy between them. "It's the strangeness of the story I can't let go of."

"Strangeness?"

He sits back in his chair with a half-agitated smile, the candlelight reflecting in his eyes. "His name was Enrique Salazar. Three years after the wreck and long after he'd been taken for dead, a Galician farmer found him walking in his fields, clean and beautifully dressed and in a complete daze. Slowly my ancestor told his story to the farmer, about the murderously overcast skies and the stiff southwesterly headwinds the ship had battled. The maps had misguided them and it had been relentless, weeks of driving weather breaking their tackle, the ship taking a great deal of water. *La Alma Verde* suddenly foundered, at least a league away from land. If you know the Blasket Sound, well, it's four square miles of violent, unpredictable sea, so it's miraculous in itself that my ancestor survived by holding on to a plank of wood and floating onto Irish headland.

"He was lying for dead on the beach when he opened his eyes and saw three women in shawls kneeling over him, touching him and conferring with one another, speaking in what must have been Irish . . . what he would come to call their 'indecipherable' language. Together the three carried him to a small boat and put him in. They rowed against the tide navigating the waves without much thought, then brought him ashore on an island, took him to a cottage with whitewashed walls and a fire burning in the hearth. They washed him and dressed him and put him to bed. He had nightmares of the hurricane-force winds, the hunger and near madness he'd suffered at sea, and when he'd awaken in a sweat, he'd always find one of the three women lying in bed beside him. At first, before he was strong again, she'd offer her breast to him to drink from. He'd lie like an infant in her care, suckling with his eyes closed, her fingers in his hair. But in time when he was healed and fortified, when he'd wake from the nightmares, he'd make love to whichever woman he found there, on and off all night, like a balm against the dreams."

She holds his eyes steadily. He blinks, then looks at the candle flame stirring in a glass box on the table. Fiona senses that he is moved. He takes a breath and continues.

"During the day he'd walk the island looking for the women, but as long as he searched, he never found them. He experienced agonizing moments when he would suddenly remember his wife and children in Andalusia. He had no sense of time, no sense of how long he was there. He'd felt it was a lifetime, and he had many children by each woman though he never saw the children and knew of them only through the pregnant states of the women at various times and because sometimes he heard children crying or laughing. He searched the island but never found them."

"Tir na mBan," Fiona says.

"What?"

"The Land of Women."

"Of women?"

"He found the Land of Women. The Irish paradise. St.

Brendan, the Irish Odysseus, was after the Land of Women when he voyaged into the western sea."

Carlos considers her words. "Enrique Salazar's life was saved but in another sense it was also ruined. When he was returned to Spain, he couldn't forget the three women. He talked about each of them to his long-suffering wife. So I don't know how it can be called paradise."

There is a moment of quiet between them, Carlos exuding a certain force and emotion.

"There is suffering in a Celtic paradise, as well as pure bliss." She is surprised at her own words, not certain where in her this thought has come from.

He considers this. "In either place, it was the other place he longed for . . ."

"And that's how you feel, isn't it, Carlos?" He is a romantic, she thinks, searching for a naive relationship with the world.

He looks at her. "Yes."

"Then you're a Celt. You have the great failing of the Celtic soul."

"What is that?"

"Nostalgia."

As they stand to go, he asks her why she had come to the antique store the previous week and she explains that she wants to open a dress shop in the front room of her house and that she had gone to Aragon's that day in search of an interesting mirror. He tells her he is going to Taos to an estate sale and that he will look for a mirror for her.

"Come by next week," he says.

She smiles. "I will."

He offers to give her a lift home but she says she feels like walking. They say a casual good-bye and she meanders awhile on the dark roads, the wind alive in the lilac trees and the Russian olives. The Santa Fe River rushes high with the melted winter snows.

She imagines Enrique Salazar passing his nights between the suffering of nightmares and the bliss he finds in the arms of whichever woman he wakes next to, each painful dream inspiring another bout of lovemaking.

That night she dreams fitfully, imagining Enrique Salazar's ship half-smashed to smithereens in jagged rock on the precipitous stretch of beach beyond the orphanage road, kittiwakes flying in and out of the broken hull. She sees it from an overlooking cliff watching the incoming waves whiten in the wind. The curragh that bears the three women comes into view through the green fog, rocking high and low on the backs of the waves. She watches them beach their small vessel in the sand and drag the wet hems of their skirts as they move through the rocks.

She opens her eyes.

On the periphery of sleep she imagines touching Carlos's naked skin. She dreams of him as a steady, enduring lover. He is Enrique Salazar and she is all three women.

She remembers her mother saying to her friend Noreen, "I have enough hunger in me for ten women." She wonders if this is her inheritance: a wildness that cannot be soothed. She had been afraid it was true that last summer in Ireland. She remembers Michael kissing her breasts, the passion between them in the barley field. For so long now she'd thought that part of her life was gone. That she'd put her hunger behind her.

She gets up and takes out the photographs of her mother from the beach of the Spanish ships. She gazes at Jane's bare arms and the areas of her long, loose dress brightened by the milky light of the sky, the sea cresting behind her, and the jutting gable of Presentation visible on the overhanging cliff.

FIVE

Even after they were situated in the blue house, Jane told Fiona stories about Presentation orphanage, about how the clothes had been taken off the back of Theresa Herlihy, a very poor girl who had died, so they might be passed on to the poverty-stricken living. Theresa was left to shiver in the next world, perished minding the church gates in nothing but her skin. Jane said that the first dress she had made at the orphanage had been with the naked dead girl in mind. She'd snuck from her dormitory and hung it outside in the middle of the night, and the next morning it was gone.

On nights when Jane thought Ronan might come, she busied herself by making dresses. She'd leave a candle in the window, sipping at a whiskey. Dressmaking kept her focused, occupied.

For a while she made the dresses furiously at night, simple dresses of heavy cloth, shifts with long sleeves. Once, with two or three whiskeys in her, Jane whispered, "Another for Theresa Herlihy." And later, lying in bed, she'd said, "It seems an awful indulgence making clothes for the living when it's the dead that are in need of them."

And it seemed always to Fiona when she was small that Jane was sewing for the dead, and so Fiona was in awe of the trappings of dressmaking, suspicious of needles and thimbles. She believed that every dress, even those commissioned for weddings, were secret tributes to Theresa Herlihy.

But her thinking changed about dressmaking when she was eleven and a young woman with an oval face and a perfect, straight nose came to commission a wedding gown. Her name was Catherine Heavey.

While Jane took her waist measurement, Catherine stood very still in only a bra and half-slip, her head bowed, arms back, as if she were about to dive into water.

It rained all the days and nights that Fiona watched Jane make Catherine Heavey's dress. An enduring drizzle, deepening for hours at a time before softening again. Turf smells had risen on the wind.

Jane had been enamored of Catherine: "She's fresh from the nuns, that girl. Such a sweet face on her."

A visit from Ronan Keane interrupted the work, and Fiona remembers seeing him asleep in her mother's narrow bed lying on his side, his back to her, like a fallen statue, the sheet like drapery around his hips and thighs. Assured by the slow, steady rhythm of his breathing, Fiona'd approached him and gingerly touched a wave of his long, red hair spread out on the pillow. It was the red of her own hair, only softer, the furl of it looser. She hadn't seen him in more than a year.

A small smile held Jane's mouth as she stood, her hair tousled, over the stove that morning, moving a piece of bread with a spatula in the frying pan.

"Hello, love," she'd said to Fiona. She was so soft Fiona could have walked through her.

Jane sat smiling with her elbows on the table, her chin on her hands, as Fiona ate. "He glimpsed you in your sleep, Fiona, and he says you're a beautiful, strong girl. He's proud at the sight of you."

Fiona tried to imagine him feeling this. His eyes were for Jane only, she thought. "The man has a shy streak in him, Fiona. He's at sea with children. But I know him to the bone," she whispered, her skin still warm with him. She leaned in close to Fiona, smiling. "To the bone," she said huskily, a flush on her. "He loves you like his own soul."

Later that day, the room dark as night with the afternoon rain, Ronan lit a candle on the table and recited to Fiona, "Little Nanny Etticoat, in a white petticoat and a red nose. The longer she stands, the shorter she grows."

He told Fiona to watch the candle grow shorter for half an hour until it looked like it had dropped its petticoats around its feet, and he disappeared into the bedroom where Jane was waiting for him.

That night in the dark kitchen, Fiona heard them whispering. He tried to disentangle himself from Jane's arms, but she'd not let him leave until she'd exacted a promise that he'd be back within a week and that they would go to the church and make things right between them.

Each day that passed without word from him, Jane grew more solemn in her labor at Catherine Heavey's dress.

Slowly over the next weeks, the proportions of the dress swelled, the train curling around the hem, forming an island of drapery.

Fiona awakened once in the middle of the night and, finding that her mother was not in bed, looked into the front room where she was asleep in her chair, still holding the threaded needle. The dress was so white, it hurt Fiona's eyes to look at it, as if it had become ignited from all its contact with Jane, a surplus of Jane's feeling having leaked out and illuminated the fabric. And its presence made the room cold, tiny white motes rising from it. It stood there facing Fiona like something exhumed from a long, primeval winter. Fiona felt afraid of it, resented its claim on her mother.

This, Fiona knew, was not a vessel to be filled by any roaming dead soul. It seemed already inhabited, to possess a will of its own. Fiona had the terrible feeling that it could see her.

The next day, because of the heavy construction of the skirts, Jane sat the dress in a chair at the kitchen table. The soft torpor of the fabric on top caused it to fall forward at the bodice and sleeves. Jane held one sleeve in her hand while piercing it again and again with the needle, insetting the little beads she called "crumbs of phosphorous" that glimmered when they trembled.

Eventually the dress was moved to their bedroom, where it

stood at the foot of their beds. Fiona remembers lying at a certain angle, squinting her eyes, so that the wall lamp looked like its head, warm and blind and catastrophic.

When Catherine Heavey came to get the dress, Jane was cautious, reminding her too sharply not to be rough getting into it.

"It's magnificent," Catherine said, her voice wavering.

Jane hunted the skirts for imperfections. "There's a bit of broken seam in the back," Jane said. "You'll leave it with me another day."

After Catherine left, Jane lay the dress across her bed. There was no broken seam.

That afternoon the weather changed. Clouds flew swiftly westward, their edges scalded by the bright head of the sun. It was warm and they left the door and windows open, allowing the wind in.

"The creature is not meant for this dress. She can't live up to it."

Jane shook her head and made a face, and Fiona wondered at what point Jane had started to dislike Catherine.

After a second whiskey Jane put Catherine's dress on. She posed before the mirror, turning at the waist, the creamy folds of the fabric shining as if they were wet. She gazed into her own eyes.

"I'll marry you," Fiona said, coming behind Jane, meeting her eyes in the mirror.

"We have each other, haven't we, love?"

"Yes," Fiona said.

But Jane's eyes drifted from Fiona's, back to her own in the mirror.

"I'll marry you," Fiona repeated until her mother pulled herself from her dream and focused again, bleary-eyed with tears and drink, on Fiona's face.

It was that day or the next that the letter from Ronan came. He was off to America, not sure when he would be back.

For a few nights Jane left the dress alone and was up late, smoking, walking in her nightgown in the potato flowers.

Jane did not let Catherine in but spoke to her at the door, saying that there'd been an accident, that she'd spilled a bottle of iodine all over the bodice. Would she like her to start another? Before the girl could answer, Jane asked her, wouldn't it be better if she went to the bridal shop in Galway, a lot of time had been lost. She handed her out the down payment: pound notes rolled and tied in a pink silk ribbon.

"I'm sorry," Jane said.

Fiona could not see Catherine's face from where she hid behind the door, but she could feel the blast of bewildered disappointment in the girl's silence.

When Catherine was gone, Jane exhaled, letting go of her imperious stance. She took everything out of the big bedroom closet, finding a place for Catherine Heavey's dress behind a curtain.

Sometimes, in the middle of the night, Fiona awakened to the light from the closet, where Jane lay on her hip embellishing the hems with beads and tiny bits of polished glass.

There would be other dresses commissioned, a series of them. Some seemed to Fiona distracted, others disappointed. Each would be slightly different, and each would eventually leave with the woman who had commissioned it. But for the time of each one's tenure, Fiona resented sharing the house with it, each one developing into a needy, ruminating sister.

Still she watched Jane cut and pin and make adjustments. Fiona was fascinated by cloth, watching it slide, patiently, rhythmically, as a seam was set. She could assess its weft and warp, appreciate its lightness or its weight.

She knew she'd have to find her own way with the quiet power of the art, inseparable as it was from womanliness.

SIX

Fiona meets with Mr. Vigil in his office on Marcy Street near the cathedral. He is more pleasant in person than over the phone, a short man with a widening middle, casually attired in a striped shirt and khaki pants. He listens politely as she tells him about her idea for the shop.

"A place where women can buy unique dresses," he says, nodding his head.

He offers her technical instruction regarding

the tricky areas of the application for the resale license, explaining the jargon to her. He tells her that she will have to fill out a new form if she hires a seamstress. And there are some more papers she will need. He can obtain them, complete them, and send them to her for her signature. He suggests a book she should read about keeping ledgers for a small business.

She leaves him, feeling encouraged.

Perusing her front room, she decides it needs new white paint. There is also a bit of cracked plasterwork in one corner. She hires a painter, Victor Jaramillo, a polite man with dark skin and silver hair who had done some work for her father. She had always liked his sad eyes and quiet seriousness.

The day he comes in to work, Victor Jaramillo brings his nephew Rudy with him to help. Rudy is in his early twenties, Fiona estimates. She feels him trying to get her attention, his light brown eyes tinged with flecks of yellow. He crosses his arms and leans back against the wall while his uncle explains to her that his plan for the day is to replaster the corner, then begin painting on the other side of the room. Rudy whistles a tune as she walks by, and when she meets his eyes, he cocks his head and smiles. She does not respond, and a palpable fog of hostility fills the room.

Unnerved, Fiona goes into the side room she has designated for sewing and closes the door. While the men work in the front room, she is determined to begin a new dress.

But gazing at the sunlight on the silver fixtures of the machine, her thoughts are in a dreamy chaos. For a while she stands without moving. With an effort of will she focuses on the fabric she intends to use, the needle poised to set a seam. She impels herself forward, and as she unravels the bolt of pale beige linen across the table, she hears Jane's voice exclaiming, taking her back again in time, "I want acres of this cloth!" The words captivate Fiona. She thinks of the acre of land in front of the blue color-washed house. Fields of Irish cloth like fields of Irish land. She imagines the dry cloth sewn with seeds and filigree. Cloth coming slowly into brocade as the potato field would come slowly into flower.

She looks at a cut of lace on the table, an intricate panel, a system of net and flower. "Irish point," she whispers, running a finger along the design. "You can barely see where the borders meet."

She tries to spread the cloth so that she can pin the pattern to it, but her arms are leaden. Her pulses start. She closes her eyes and realizes she cannot separate the idea of working cloth from the idea of tilling Irish earth, and lace from the frothy tides that rushed at its edges. She sees the implements of sewing as miniature plows and tractors, rakes and spades. She cannot imagine the dresses she once made coming to life in dry New Mexico air.

She sits slowly and hangs her head. She is no longer the eighteen-year-old Irish girl who sewed lavish dresses, her powers as a seamstress as hopelessly lost as that last Irish summer; the summer of excess when the bog lilies overran the swamp and dog roses clotted the roadsides. She sees in her memory the long Spanish needle she once used to embroider seed pearls into satin.

All day she remains sitting with her realization, looking at the dressworks to the sound of the men working in the other room.

In the morning when Victor Jaramillo and his nephew arrive, she almost wants to send them away, though the job is only half-finished. They come in and take up again with their work.

She goes to her bedroom and closes the door. She looks noncommittally at the book Mr. Vigil suggested she read. In the hall outside her room she hears Rudy singing, *"Lo mucho que te quiero . . ."*

He goes into the bathroom but does not completely close the door, and she can hear him pissing. She thinks he must be directing his spray in such a way as to make it louder, enjoying the thought of her discomfort.

An hour later, she goes into the kitchen and turns on the faucet to get a drink of water. Sensing something, she turns suddenly and finds him standing two feet behind her. She drops the glass.

"Shit!" she screams.

Gravity overcomes his expression. "I'm sorry," he says.

"This room is off-limits to you!" she cries. She storms out to Victor Jaramillo. "Your nephew thinks he can wander freely around my house."

Furrows deepen on the older man's forehead. He gives Rudy a furious look.

"Can you please explain to him that the back of the house is off-limits to him?" she cries.

"Yes, I'm sorry, miss."

Fiona stands there breathing hard with anger. "I'd like you both to leave now for the day," she says suddenly.

Mr. Jaramillo looks taken aback. "He won't go back there again, miss!"

"Please come back to finish tomorrow, Mr. Jaramillo," Fiona says. "Please come alone."

Rudy looks at her, his eyes golden now with anger.

She senses the older man's disapproval, and for a moment

she doubts herself, but she holds her ground, crossing her arms. She just wants them gone.

As they put things away, the two men argue softly and intensely in Spanish. She goes to her room, waiting for them to leave. She hears the truck door slam twice outside and the engine start. She walks out again, ladders still standing, tarps left spread.

The air simmers faintly with the heat and odor of their sweat, but in a few minutes the house grows serene again.

She sits in the wicker chair. The anger, tight a moment ago in her chest, dissolves into frustrated confusion.

Gazing at the mild sunlight on the wall, her feelings give way to sadness. She thinks of Presentation orphanage, and finds herself there, rushing through its decrepit avenues. She knows the labyrinthine paths as if she has roamed them many times.

She hears her own excited breathing as she ascends a forbidden staircase to a height where girls are not allowed.

Arriving at the threshold of the upper floor, she peers into the abode of the nuns, her heartbeat amplified now. The climate and the quality of the light are more silvery this high, and she knows that this is because it is closer to the clouds.

The nuns are all in the chapel at vespers, yet the air up here buzzes with the perpetual residue of prayer. She trespasses into the hallway, counting three doors to Sister Delphine's cell. Inside the austere little room she struggles to open a small, locked cedar box she finds there, hoping to discover some bit of memorabilia from the nun's past. Some clue to her private heart. But the box does not give. She puts it down and dances in a circle with her arms up in the air before throwing herself onto the cot and embracing the thin, flat pillow in its rough-hewn case, smelling it greedily for a trace of Sister Delphine's odor.

Fiona pulls herself from the daydream, panting, feeling feverish. She knows she was not asleep, and she struggles to comprehend the nature of what she has just experienced. She sits forward and understands. This particular memory is not hers at all, but Jane's. She does not know how she comes to keep it for her.

For so long she has kept an image of Jane petrified as if in amber, caught midswim in her own anxiety. She ventures with a palpitating heart to soften to her, to go closer. She sits back in the chair again, and fixes her eyes to the sunlit wall, returning to a corridor of the orphanage.

She moves slowly, cautiously, turning corners until she comes upon Jane as a girl standing in the half-light, wearing a simple bleached-white dress, her eyes quizzical, worried. She regards Fiona, then turns slowly from her, her dress leaving a streak of whiteness as she moves away. Fiona gazes after her as if she is gazing at a wayward younger sibling.

Fiona sits forward, shaking herself from the half-dream, wiping tears and sweat from her face. She struggles to remember Jane as a mother. She knows she used to curl against Jane's body, rest her head upon her shoulder or her breast, bask in her surrounding heat. But she can only see the girl in the half-light. There is no mother whose body was her original abode. Jane the mother falls away like the flat in Athlone does, or the blue color-washed house. Insubstantial. Easily given to ruin.

These thoughts hurt Fiona, even as they connect her unfathomably to her mother.

She gets up and moves about the room now, agitated. She is tired of being so rigid against remembering.

That last summer keeps a secret from her, holds some sadness in abeyance. She cannot recall the facts, the course of events that led to a terrible fall from grace.

But she must go further back to understand. Ned McGinty, she thinks. It all begins with Ned McGinty.

SEVEN

When they'd first moved into the blue house, Jane had discovered that their bit of land bordered the McGinty farm. Ned McGinty, Jane told Fiona, had once been in love with her.

Both Ned and his old mother, Attracta McGinty, who lived with him, were unfriendly. The old woman gave them hostile looks, while Ned ignored them.

Jane waved at Ned anyhow, across the fence.

Once, when his mother was not with him, Jane called out to him in a pleading voice, and the big man had relented and given her a nod.

"I hurt that man," Jane told Fiona one day as they walked past the McGinty property. "I broke his heart."

Fiona learned that Ned had courted Jane when she was still with the nuns. Even after Jane had met Ronan Keane, Ned had come around. When Jane thought of Ned, she got a peevish, regretful look on her face. Once when they'd run into him in Roundstone, he and Jane having accidentally come face-to-face, he'd looked gravely at her and she'd crimsoned with shame.

She'd go quiet when she saw him. She'd get a far-off look.

Fiona was fourteen years old the day she and Jane saw Ned McGinty walking on the side of the road in heavy rain. They were driving back to Roundstone from Galway.

Jane honked the car horn and stopped for him. They'd seen his truck broken down a ways back.

"Get in, Ned!" Jane cried. He looked into the small car, hesitating, and she said, "*In!*"

He climbed into the back, settling his big legs, cramped by the seat and slamming the door, filling the car with a smell of wet sheep.

As if they were in the habit of talking, Jane went on to him about the dear price of the fabric she'd just bought. "I threw caution to the wind today, Ned," she cried effusively. "Have you ever had a day where you did a thing like that? Throw caution to the four winds?" Fiona cringed at the high pitch of her voice.

He breathed uncomfortably behind them like a ram caught in a hutch and ready to bolt. Fiona looked at him in the rearview mirror, a big-boned man with a day's blondish growth on his red, wet face, hair plastered by the rain to his forehead; handsomeish but dull behind the eyes, she thought. He caught her eye and then averted his, staring out at passing fields.

"Ned!" Jane cried. "Do you remember way back when I was still with the nuns, the time I saw you chasing the black cow through Mrs. Hanratty's pansies?" The flush was risen in her cheeks. "Do you remember it, Ned?"

Fiona watched the eyes that avoided hers. They lit up faintly. "Aye," he said.

"What was her name? That sweet rogue of a black cow?"

"Mercy."

"Yes, and wasn't Sister John on and on about the blasphemy of naming a cow Mercy?"

"Yes."

"And you named her that yourself, did you not, Ned?"

"Aye," he said, brought out of himself a bit. "You remember that, do you, Jane?"

"I do, of course."

At that, Fiona saw a bit of resistance gone from his face.

Jane stopped the engine and they both got out and stood together at the side of the car talking. She laughed with unnatural animation and touched his chest. He wore a little smile, restrained at the corners of his mouth.

Fiona felt her own face burn with embarrassment.

When he left, Jane got in the car, breathing hard with a certain resolve, watching him walk away.

"Ned McGinty is a handsome figure of a man. Is he not, Fiona?"

Jane's friend Noreen Feeney had told them that he was a dyed-in-the-wool bachelor.

"A man who lives with his mother," Fiona said.

Jane was quiet, pressing her lips together.

That evening as Fiona washed the dishes, she listened to Jane struggling to persuade Noreen Feeney that she had a shot at Ned McGinty.

"Old Irene Dunne married that other dyed-in-the-wool bachelor," Jane said.

Two years earlier, Fiona had helped Jane make Irene Dunne's wedding dress. The gown was one of the most elaborate that they'd ever made. Irene, middle-aged and overweight, had insisted on being heavily corseted, and getting her into it had been something of a fiasco.

"Tom Delaney," Noreen said. "She married Tom Delaney."

"Yes."

"Eight years it took her to snag that big stiff of a fella, if it was a day."

"But she did it and she's years older than me. And nothing at all to look at. At least I have that," Jane said, waiting for some affirmation from her friend, who only looked down her nose and drew at her cigarette. Noreen was a dour-looking woman, narrow about the face and shoulders. The redness of her lipstick accentuated the downiness of her upper lip.

"And she was no prize in the personality department either," Jane added.

"But she had a bit of money saved, Jane. She had that to offer old Tom. And at a time when he needed it something desperate."

"Oh," Jane said, and looked pensively around the room.

Noreen tapped her ashes on her saucer and laughed, as if

she sensed Jane's determination and it irritated her. "I couldn't believe that wedding gown you made her! Old Irene Dunne rigged up in satin! Like a dung beetle in a silk purse."

Fiona held the rag still on the plate she was washing and waited to hear how her mother would respond. But there was silence, and the animosity in Noreen's tone intensified. "That frigate of a dress she sailed to the altar in. Could you have made it any wider, Jane? She thought she was the queen of England. The Kearney boy bowed down and called her 'Your Majesty,' and the stupid cow took it as a compliment."

Fiona slammed the plate she was washing down on the counter. Her eyes met Noreen's and held them.

"She's at that age, Jane. Watch out for her," Noreen said, pointing her chin at Fiona.

Jane glanced with irritation at Fiona, then seemed to forget her. Jane drew in a distressed breath and slowly exhaled, lost in her thoughts.

Noreen held out awhile before blurting out, "He goes to the Moon and the Stars every Friday night."

"Does he?"

"As religiously as he eats every meal with his mother and stays in every night of the week to listen to the wireless with her. For a while he danced with Bitty Connelly, but she got tired of him. He's a stick-in-the-mud. Now he just stands and drinks a pint watching the couples dance. He looks like he wants to dance, but he hasn't got the backbone to ask anyone." Noreen took a sip of tea, then clucked her tongue. "You've got your work cut out for you."

"Will you come with me this Friday?" Jane asked.

"I'll go with you Friday," Noreen said. "We'll get gussied

up. Though I've no illusions myself about any of the bounders that go there."

When Noreen left that night, Fiona tried to sleep. Sipping on a whiskey, Jane came in and sat on the edge of her bed.

"He was besotted with me once, Fiona. Besotted with me!" Jane bent into herself as if she could not contain the exhilaration of the feeling.

"He came every evening before vespers and stood outside behind the iron bars of the gate. Sometimes I pretended I didn't see him there and I hummed and danced in the darkening light and I felt his eyes on me, watching me with adulation. He was loving me with his eyes.

"I pressed my face out between the bars once and kissed him on the mouth. And every night I met him out there, the two of us pressing our bodies to the bars trying to get as close to each other as we could.

"He begged me to marry him and I said that when the nuns released me from that prison, I'd marry him straightaway. He gave me a bracelet with the faces of martyrs in little glass lozenges.

"I'd laughed at him and said, 'You don't woo a girl, you oaf, by giving her a bracelet of martyrs.' But I took it anyhow and I have it still.

"And then the summer's day came when I scaled the iron bars headed for the beach and came upon Ronan Keane." Jane quieted, looking down and shaking her head slowly. "And after that day, I didn't go out to Ned anymore. From the high window in Presentation, I saw him waiting on me outside, every night. But I didn't go to him."

Fiona was quiet.

"If you knew the power I had over the man once. I'm still a

young woman." With a sudden tearful defiance Jane said, "I'll not waste myself.

"And I still have my attractiveness, don't I?" she asked, trying to extract from Fiona what she could not from Noreen.

"Yes," Fiona said grudgingly.

"Ah, love." Jane touched Fiona's hair.

"What would you talk about with him?"

"What's between a man and a woman isn't about talking."

Fiona turned away from her.

"I like the look o' him and the sound of his voice. And he remembers me all lit up in myself. Ned has the memory of me from that time. God forgive me, Fiona, but I need to have a man desire me." Jane looked down thoughtfully at her hands in her lap. "I remember the feeling of it. God on earth! That time, so short-lived in my life, but the very brightest spot in it."

"But Ned McGinty is so . . . so stiff."

"But he's the kind of man who'd come home every night to us."

Jane got in bed a little while, sighing and turning restlessly until she got up in the dark and disappeared for a long time. Fiona saw the light on in the lavatory, the door ajar. She tiptoed over and peered in.

Jane was standing before the bathroom mirror with her blouse open, gazing at herself.

Jane went into town and bought three Valencia oranges, the juice of which she added to batter and frosting for a cake, which she and Fiona brought to Mrs. McGinty.

"I'm Jane O'Faolain, Mrs. McGinty, and this is my daughter, Fiona. We're on the property bordering your own."

Mrs. McGinty focused on Jane through a pair of cloudy glasses. "I know damn well who you are."

"Well, I thought I might make a fresh start of things, Mrs. McGinty," Jane said.

The old woman eyed the cake and said, "I don't eat frosted cake."

"Oh," Jane said. "I see."

The old woman closed the door.

"Jayz, what an old bitch!" Fiona said.

"Well, she doesn't eat frosted cake, Fiona," Jane said.

A few days later Jane tried with a chocolate loaf dusted in powdered sugar, but was turned away again. She told Fiona she might make a Vienna loaf and leafed through her recipe book, but was sufficiently put off by the old woman not to attempt it again.

It was around this same time, when Fiona was fourteen, that the first checks came from Ronan in America. He'd made a success of himself as a photographer in the Southwest. Jane stopped taking commissions, living exclusively on the money that he sent, along with the programs of all his exhibitions and copies of some of his photographs, mostly of the dry, reddish-looking landscapes and vast mountain ranges, strange, unearthly-looking places in bright sun and black shadows. In one exhibition he'd taken photographs exclusively of clouds. In the program there was a picture of the dedication card that had been posted on the wall in the gallery. "These photographs are dedicated to my daughter, Fiona, in Ireland."

She had been moved and filled with wonder over it. She wrote back to him expressing her admiration for the pictures.

Thereafter he always addressed to her the packages he sent and included a note or a letter for her.

She wrote to him once that she had dreams of one day traveling. He invited her to come and visit whenever she liked; she had her own claim on him. Jane was unnerved by it all, and one day Fiona found a letter sent to her from Ronan, opened. Jane said she hadn't opened it, that it had come that way.

"Liar!" Fiona had cried.

"He comes around now when you need him the least!"

"Oh! I always thought it was you who needed him. I didn't know that I ever got to need him!"

Jane looked stunned by those words. She stared at the floor in front of her, struggling with her thoughts.

"Don't ever open my mail again!" Fiona cried defiantly.

The fury she felt exhilarated her. Her correspondence with Ronan became a kind of refuge, and she took pleasure in keeping it from Jane. Sometimes she took out the program from the exhibition and read and reread his dedication to her.

Jane's pursuit of Ned McGinty intensified during the years of Fiona's adolescence. But beyond the Friday nights dancing at the Moon and the Stars, things did not progress much between them.

Whenever Jane ran into him on the road or saw him in his field, he nodded but never went out of his way to come up and speak with her. He behaved like an acquaintance, and it never ceased to surprise and disappoint Jane.

One Friday night when Fiona was sixteen, she went with Ann Finley, a girl she knew from school, to the Moon and the Stars to see what it was like, neither of them ever having been to a dance hall.

The floor was dim and crowded with couples, Jane and Ned among them. Three musicians played on a stage illuminated by a string of bright colored lights.

A heavyset woman in a green dress stepped forward with a microphone and sang:

> *Feather beds are soft*
> *and painted rooms are sunny*
> *but I would leave them all*
> *for to go with my love, Johnny.*

The singer stepped back into a shadow, wiping sweat from her brow as a fiddler stepped forward and played a riff. While most couples danced vivaciously, Jane and Ned clung to each other, eyes closed as if they were alone in the room. The side of Jane's face was pressed to Ned's collar, and Ned's face rested against the top of Jane's head.

Fiona had not thought they would be like that. She'd thought she'd see Ned maudlin as usual, evasive and half-dancing. But they were so set on each other, so in sync, as if they were two parts of the same whole. And Fiona thought, "It's finally happened. It won't be long now."

But the next day Fiona was with Jane when they spotted Ned driving his sheep. Jane waved and Ned looked at her stone-faced giving her half a nod.

Fiona felt as if a hand had clapped her hard against the chest. She touched Jane's arm and said, "I saw the two of you dancing last night."

"Yes," Jane said.

"He was besotted with you," Fiona said, perplexed.

"Yes, it's that way with us every Friday until the moment

the last note plays in the last song. But in the bright of morning it might as well have all been a dream."

She slept little most nights, attending the dress once meant for Catherine Heavey, which had increased and complicated into something that could have been called magnificent, skirts held wide with a cagework bell, which Jane had constructed with panniers of linen and cane. Even after the skirts were frothy with layers, Jane made additions of every imaginable kind. Glinting beads of glass, or even of plastic if they caught the light beautifully. She drilled holes in tiny seashells and sewed those on as well. Her eye was always open for phosphorescence.

But Fiona was nauseated by the dress, which brushed at the walls of the closet like some ornate, hybrid lily growing in the dark, at once reluctant of the light and starved for it, shivering when it sparkled. Fiona called it the Giantess, impossible creature that it was.

Yet she found herself drawn to the drawers and shelves of Jane's sewing supplies. Random cuts of velvet, bits of ribbon and silk, seemed to shimmer with possibilities. Even hooks and eyes, snaps and clasps, seemed talismanic, darkly sacred. One day in the late spring when she was seventeen, she found among the ribbons a swatch of silk so soft that it felt wet.

She kept it with her, moving it between her fingers in her pocket. She took it to bed with her and held it to her mouth, breathing on it until it was as warm as her own skin. One day she located the bolt of silk it had originally been cut from. She was alone in the house and free to unravel it over the kitchen table.

As she pressed her palms to it, she heard a knock on the door. She opened it to the hired man, Mr. Ryan, accompanied by a tall, dark-haired boy a few years older than herself, a boy with a striking face she'd seen once before in town. She knew he was not from Roundstone.

Mr. Ryan wanted to speak to Jane, but Fiona explained that she was probably down in the dairy, milking Oonagh, the cow.

"This is my nephew, Michael," he said. "Michael, Fiona."

His dark hair was long and he tossed his head to get it out of his eyes. He smiled at her.

"Do you mind if I wait for you here?" Michael asked his uncle.

Mr. Ryan gave him a wry look.

"Can you give me a cup of tea?" Michael asked Fiona. She nodded, and as Mr. Ryan headed down the hill, Michael stepped into the house.

While she made him the tea, he stood looking at the dressform and the piece of silk lying across the table. She turned to face him, her heart going.

"You're a dressmaker," he said.

She said nothing, but watched his eyes.

"Did you ever read the *Odyssey*?"

"No."

"I'm reading it at school," he said. "One of the islands Odysseus visits belongs to the goddess Circe. She's a spinner, a dressmaker. You're on your own little isle up here on this hill. And those are alder trees down near the road, aren't they?"

"Yes, I think so."

"Circe's isle is surrounded by alder trees, too." He smiled.

He walked over to the dressform and touched the curve between the waist and the hip; then he looked at Fiona. "This is set to your own figure, isn't it?" He gazed at Fiona's body. His boldness appalled and thrilled her. She felt a shiver on her own waist where he touched the dressform.

She cleared the silk from the table and set down his tea. He took a drink of it. "Circe turned men into animals. Her whole island was crawling with men who she had enchanted into various creatures, all wretched and salivating."

She stood facing him, in wonder over his words. Mr. Ryan called to him suddenly from outside. He drank the hot tea in a few drafts, nodded to her, and descended the hill, turning once as he did and waving at her.

She took off her clothes and stared at herself in the mirror.

She saw a pale, invisible dress forming itself like ectoplasm around her dips and curves, mutable, sexual; a kind of gossamer clothing that imagined itself there and then disappeared. That night she made her first dress and hung it out on the line. In the morning it was gone, but she found it later in a clump on the roadside. "'Twas only the wind that took it!" she said to herself. She was actually glad. No dead girls waited for her dresses. She could disregard her mother's superstitions and flee at last, from childhood.

The world felt beautiful and odd to her. She stood in the alder trees letting the wind fuss insistently over her, lifting locks of her hair, sweeping it this way and that.

She walked at night in the ineffable air, stunned by the masses of moonlit clouds, the swift way they banked together crossing the night sky. She was Circe, the dressmaker, who turned men into animals.

Standing at the fence near the McGinty yard, she was drawn to the ram bucking at the boards of its pen, its eyes on the ewe who moved at ease through new grass. She dreamed of barking wolves restlessly patrolling around the house, whining for her to come out.

*

Thereafter Fiona took secret pleasure in making a sleeve or a bodice, hiding her fraught little workings from Jane until she had all the pieces ready to put together on a form. She was amazed at how naturally the craft came to her and how different her own hand was from her mother's. There was no torpor or disappointment in the dresses she made, her seams so snugly sewn that the fabric at the sleeves and skirts seemed to bloom out from the waist, lifting jauntily.

She read the *Odyssey*. About Circe, who sang to her loom and drugged Odysseus' hungry sailors, transforming them into swine, leaving them to wallow. When Circe tried to transform Odysseus into an animal and he remained unenchanted, she fell in love with him. He would not meet her amorous advances until she'd turned his men back into human beings and he'd exacted a promise from her not to plot any more mischief against him.

But it was Calypso with whom Fiona truly identified. Calypso, who was more the girl, less ruthless and mature in her power than Circe, and more isolated than Circe, who lived with her many seamstresses and servants.

Calypso lived in a glorious cave surrounded by thickets of alder, black poplar, and cypresses. In this idyllic place streams crossed iris meadows, with horned owls and falcons and sea crows in the leaves. Lovely Calypso had welcomed the exhausted Odysseus as he stumbled ashore alone. She fed him and gave him heady drink and shared her bed with him, offering him immortality and ageless youth. And he stayed with her for years, but eventually tired of her embraces, restless to be again on his way.

This ending between them filled Fiona with anxiety.

Odysseus was a wanderer, she reminded herself. He was human and moved through the dangers of the world. Yet the goddesses, held to their paradisal islands, struck Fiona as sadder, hungrier beings.

On the night of her eighteenth birthday, Fiona waited on Jane to come home. Every year there was a surprise, a gift of some sort. And Jane would make a trifle or a cake and they would both eat too much of it.

But when Jane came in, she was with Bitty Connelly and Lucy Deane, two of the single women who also frequented the Moon and the Stars on Friday nights. They'd just come from the pub.

Jane had offered to make them all a fry.

Fiona hesitated at her sewing. Lucy Deane glanced at her with eyes made bleary with alcohol and said, "She's certainly the good one, isn't she?"

Fiona stiffened and left the room, but from the bedroom she could still hear the frying of the sausages and the laughter and the small talk that went on among the three of them. Jane was a little drunk and boisterous, laughing loudly and at almost anything.

"So," Fiona heard Lucy say, "that photograph there taken on the beach. That's you, is it, Jane?"

"Yes," Jane said, a trace of hurt in her voice that Lucy had to ask.

"Jayz, ye looked the beauty then."

The sausages sizzled.

"Was that taken by Fiona's father? What was his name?"

"Ronan."

"That bastard, that dog that ran out on you."

"I have no regrets. Not a single one. I'd do it all again in the wink of an eye."

"Ye keep that picture awfully close to the shrine of the Virgin Mary."

"Let's put it this way," Jane said. "If I'd put up one of the photographs taken half an hour later, it'd be a blasphemy to the purity of Our Lady." They all cackled.

"Jane," Lucy said, "Noreen says the old bugger McGinty won't even give you a dip of the wick!"

Fiona heard the huff of the fire go out under the burner. The sizzling quieted. With a forced lightness Jane said, "Not true. The things that happened between myself and that man last Friday night would make a tinker pink."

"Oh, Jayzus! Tell us!" cried Bitty.

"For the love of God!" Lucy said.

"That man turns me into butter of spreading consistency!" Fiona heard her mother say.

They laughed.

"Tell us about the cock on him!" Lucy cried.

"Sssshh," Jane cried. "The girl will hear you."

"Tell us!"

"He's got the cock of a donkey, for the love of Christ," Jane said in a hushed voice.

"It must hurt something fierce!" Bitty said.

"Only until I got used to it, and then we were at it like hares!" Jane said. "I'm surprised the springs of the truck seat were still intact when we'd finished."

They squealed and laughed.

As Jane dished out the sausages, Fiona peered out the door and saw Lucy and Bitty exchange a conspiratorial smirk, confirming her suspicion that they were making her mother the butt of a joke. They knew damn well that she'd had no tangle with Ned McGinty.

Jane brought them platefuls of sausages and eggs, and between mouthfuls Lucy said, "When a man does a woman that hard, he owes her a walk down the aisle, Jane. I've brought you a bottle of Lourdes water. A friend of mine just did the pilgrimage."

Jane looked up and saw Fiona watching them but dismissed her, excited at the appearance of the holy water. She put down her fork and wiped a smear of egg off her upper lip.

"Sprinkle it on his shoulder the next time he dances with you, Jane," Bitty said.

"Or drink it down yourself and invoke the Holy Mother!" Lucy said, elbowing Bitty.

"Ah, sure," Jane said. "If it'll work, I'll try it."

They all laughed, Jane harder than the other two.

It was widely known, the things Jane'd already done; visiting holy wells, leaving little offerings of jewels and swatches of wedding lace. These two women encouraged it, always suggesting another "tried-and-true" charm for catching a man. Jane had even gone as far as to lie to Ned, telling him that she had a large nest egg in the bank, saying wasn't it a lot of land they had between the two of them? With the fences knocked down it would be the biggest farm in Roundstone. But even that hadn't worked.

"How could you let them make an ass of you so?" Fiona cried after the women left.

"Leave off on me, for the love of God, Fiona," Jane said, and left the kitchen a mess.

A few minutes later she passed from the lavatory into the

bedroom wearing her nightgown. When Fiona heard the springs of Jane's bed, she cried out, "Do you expect me to clean up after you?"

"I'll come," Jane said.

Fiona stood gazing at her own reflection in the chrome teapot when she saw Jane moving in behind her. Fiona moved angrily away and Jane's body rocked slightly at the rejection.

On the floor near the table Fiona saw some fallen cigarette ash, and a wild flare of anger rose up in her. Other things made the anger catch and intensify: the egg stain on the napkin Jane had used; Jane's shoes left in front of the door so they'd have to be kicked out of the way before the door could be opened.

Fiona went into the bedroom while Jane did the washing up. She whispered into her hands, "I hate her. I hate Jane O'Faolain." She felt mighty as if she were glowing and a little dizzy. As if she'd been hyperventilating.

Ann Finley had an aunt in Galway who ran a millinery shop and was looking for an assistant. Fiona had kept the address on a folded piece of paper in her drawer. She took out a pen and paper and sat at the kitchen table beginning a letter to Ann's aunt.

"What is that?"

"A letter to Ann Finley's aunt in Galway, about a job," Fiona said, looking hard at her. "I'm eighteen now. I can leave."

Jane stopped breathing. "Oh, Christ, Fiona. Your birthday."

Fiona moved her pen with purpose.

"Can ye forgive me, love?"

When Fiona did not answer, Jane hesitated, then went back to the press to put a spoonful of dry tea into the pot. When the tea was made, she sat at the table across from Fiona, who bent over the page pretending to be deeply engaged.

After a minute Fiona looked up. Jane gazed sadly at her, as if from across a chasm.

Fiona looked down again quickly at the letter she'd begun, surprised by the anger her mother's look inspired in her.

"You wouldn't go and work in Galway, would you?" Jane asked softly.

"Don't interrupt me!" Fiona cried.

There was silence. Fiona put her hand over her forehead, shielding her eyes as if to close out Jane's presence as she worked. A minute passed and Jane said, "You've a lovely talent with the dresses, Fiona."

Fiona banged her pencil down on the table. "I'll do this in the bedroom!"

"No," Jane said, more depleted than perturbed. "I'll go in there. I've work I want to do anyhow," a reference to her own impossible dress.

Fiona sat up for an hour with the letter, and when it was finished, she heaved a sigh, her anger at Jane now diminished. She stood and opened the door. A new smell was in the air that evening. Mr. Ryan had plowed the two fields in front of the house and they were black, ready for seeding. She put the pages inside the envelope, sealed it, put on postage, and left it conspicuously on the table. When she looked in on her, Jane was still on the floor before the Giantess, the hems riddled with multifaceted embroideries.

Fiona went outside and stopped before an enclosed field where a young stallion had been let loose with a young mare, both jogging around, rearing up and whinnying. She stood at the fence and watched them, entranced. The mare was saucy and nervous and lithe. The stallion had muscular hips and a long middle when he stood on his hind legs, screeching, nodding his head, pawing with his front hooves.

The mare, who was lovely with light tan mane and tail and a dark brown body, ejected the roan stallion every time he tried to ride her.

The more Fiona watched them circle each other, the more she sensed that the mare didn't really want to win, but that she wanted the stallion to be surer of himself and to overcome her. The stallion stood away from the mare and screeched at her, tension in his lips and nostrils. His insistence was important to the game. He had to rise to the occasion of her; to meet the challenge.

She thought of bold Michael Devlin.

Fiona moves away from the memory. She is still sitting on the bed. It is almost dark now and the shadows in her room startle her.

She takes a breath and reaches out, switches on the lamp.

She is on the verge of reconstructing that last spring and summer now. Did she ever send that letter to Ann Finley's aunt? she asks herself. No. It was as if she had known even as she'd written it that her life was about to open. She had felt it that night in her skin, the volition of the fields waiting for the seed, the fecund darkness aching to burst into green.

She remembers going home from watching the horses and tossing the letter into the rubbish, the address getting slowly defaced by the shavings of carrots and potatoes.

EIGHT

Fiona knows as she looks at the place from outside that no one is at Aragon's. She pulls at the massive wooden door and it creaks open, admitting her. Her eyes struggle to adjust to the dark, the faces of La Trinidad, the triplet Christs, confronting her from the baroque, interior twilight.

The air deeper in is still and contained and her presence causes echoes as she descends the stairs to Carlos's work area. The figure of the girl in the green dress leans forward in the penumbra. Fiona can see that Carlos has been working on her hand, reconstructing it. It is still wet with some solution. She looks into the figure's eyes, which give the impression of intense reverie. The girl's heart is somewhere else, far away, alive in a past, more vital life.

Fiona thinks for a moment that Carlos possesses some profound faculty of the soul. How did he resuscitate this figure? He has gently brought her out of her degradation, restored her to an older, purer obsession; to her original self. Four hundred years and thousands of miles between himself and this monument, yet he searched her out and found her. What is four hundred years to a monument? she asks herself.

Fiona notices a door in the wall, which she approaches and opens. A lamp, very much like the storm lanterns she and Jane used in Ireland, hangs on an iron hook impaled into the wall, a box of kitchen matches on top of it. She lifts the top and lights the cloth wick and closes it again. She descends a narrow flight of stairs, her footsteps echoing behind her as if slower replicas of herself were following in the dark, concentrating themselves in the closeness of the vault.

At the bottom she enters a room with lights running along the walls. But she cannot figure out how to turn them on. It is a kind of study, a desk piled with papers, a bulletin wall upon which documents and pictures are pinned. Along one wall she finds a system of tiny marked drawers. She opens a few, holding the lamp up to each one. Bits of broken pottery, stones; warped, partially defaced coins; odd bits of broken jewelry. The finger of a statue. He is obsessed with objects that have survived time.

Piles of worn books three and four feet high crowd a corner. Books about the Armada, about shipwrecks and underwater archaeology. The history of Spain. Galicia. Ireland. The lonely isles of the Irish west. Sixteenth-century Spanish boatbuilding. Opening books randomly, she finds margins heavily marked, notes throughout.

She yearns to know why his ancestor's story inspires such passion, puts him so inexhaustibly at its service.

She moves deeper into the room, discovering large objects under glass, some wrapped in plastic.

She holds her lamp close to a glass box that encloses a heavy, ornate cross, an orgy of gold filigree around a central jewel, maybe an emerald, streaked within, a phantom blotting its otherwise clear, green perfection.

A heavy sword hangs from a hook on the wall. Its edges are dull, but the handle is elaborately decorated. Fiona tries to imagine the powerful arm that could wield such a weapon. These two objects are emblematic of war, of politics, yet each emanates a kind of patience.

Pinned to the wall above the sword are a series of cards and photographs. One depicts a man rigged up in diver's gear, gracefully suspended, one pointed flipper almost touching the seafloor, fronds and filigree of plant life in midsway stirred by the man's presence, stream from a wreckage of what looks like archaic lamps and iron wheels and utensils.

The man holds the heavy cross to his chest, filaments of sand falling from it, creating a fog as if he has just unblanketed it from its four-hundred-year-old bed. Fiona knows that the man is Carlos, thinking he has found Enrique Salazar's ship. And that the ocean is the Atlantic, off the western coast of Ireland.

In one photograph Carlos is swimming downward at an angle, his body above him; he is reaching for something that lies in a heap of sand, his hands stirring the silt of the ocean floor. Descent is more magical than ascent, she thinks.

What is it like, she yearns to ask him, to touch the seafloor?

In a glass box on a long table, she is startled by the bodice of a dress, old and half eaten away. Attached to a crumbling, crenellated fabric, a pair of lace sleeves and a lace collar. She knows the lace. It's Irish. Youghal lace, she is certain. Holding the lamp near, she looks closely at the damage, very fine threads broken from the warp. Such a thing she knows cannot be restored. She wonders what this could mean to him, that he has it sequestered in this box, the living process of disintegration held in suspension.

A worn map of Spain is on the wall, folded open only at the northwest coast. The crumples on the paper look like hills or dips and rises in the land. Fiona imagines this map having traveled with Carlos, kept warm in his pocket next to his chest, being taken out to consult in the Spanish wind. But this lace, she knows, is Irish.

She runs her finger along a particular fold in the map and reads the place names he has circled: "Noia, Lobeira, Sada, Moana." Like women's names. Some have been circled twice. He was once restless for these places.

Going back toward the door, she looks at the bulletin board over the desk and notices a map of Ireland upon which he has drawn graphs over the Blasket Sound. A small X is marked in one place where the lines intersect. He has written in a tiny hand, *The Maria Christina.*

There at his desk, scribbled notes probably written recently: *Forty miles north of the Blasket Sound? La Alma Verde.* The disarray of his papers, his written calculations and graphs, some erased many times over, are still charged with his struggle, his excitement. Catching her breath and looking around her, she begins to realize the inappropriateness of her trespassing.

She leaves the room, carrying the lamp. The air and light change profoundly as she reaches the summit of the stairs, blows out the flame, and returns the lamp to the place where she found it. When she turns around, she sees Carlos standing near the figure in green. She feels his confusion on the air between them. His expression becomes sober.

"I came to see you," she says apologetically.

He says nothing.

"The door was open," she says nervously.

Still he says nothing and she knows he knows she's lying.

She breathes out audibly. "I'm sorry."

She takes a few steps toward him. "That old lace dress you have. That's not Spanish lace. It's Irish."

"I know," he says quietly.

She lets go a breath, glad that he knows. Moved that he knows.

"I came," she says, hearing the appeal in her voice, "to invite you out for a drink."

They walk silently together down the narrow, dry descent toward the Hacienda Rancho de Chimayo, the gravel crunching underfoot, the lowering sun igniting the earth-colored walls, deep shadows falling from the sides of houses. She senses his mood toward her gradually changing, more open to her moment by moment, perhaps curious about the intimacy her violation has afforded them, her close inspection of the vault of his obsessions.

Now and then as they continue on their way he casts a look at her. Once she reads a trace of voluptuousness in his expression.

"I didn't find an interesting mirror for your dress shop at that estate sale. I looked for one for you."

"Oh," she says, having forgotten about it. "That's all right." She almost tells him that she doubts that the dress shop will happen at all, but the thought of explaining it all exhausts her.

"I'm going to Ireland tomorrow," he says.

Her breath freezes in her chest. Her heart waits. "You are?"

"On a dive. My friend Gaston thinks he knows where *La Alma Verde* can be found, at a new location further north. He thinks it may have been recorded under the wrong name, *La Vela de Maria,* a ship mentioned in no other historical record."

"The Candle of Mary," Fiona muses. As they are entering the doors to the Hacienda, she notices him studying the freckled skin of her arm. It hits her that he has tolerated her intrusion because she is Irish. She memorizes his examining look, the way he studies the surface of her as she has just studied the Youghal lace. She dislikes him for it and wonders if he thinks of her as one of his refugee finds. She suddenly feels lonely in his company.

But as they are following the hostess to an outside table, a dark Hispanic woman passing them touches Carlos's arm.

"Carlos," she says.

His eyes narrow. He nods at her but does not smile. They continue on and he seems irritated by the encounter, as if the woman has provoked something in him that threatens to distract him.

They are seated at a table on a high plateau of land overlooking the patio. A waiter with a white tunic lights the candle in its clear votive glass and they order wine.

Around the adobe walls that surround the patio, poplars and tamarisks stir. The red-streaked clouds of dusk have moved off to the west, and the dark evening blue sky is not yet black. The smell of burning piñon wafts up from the mud fireplace inside through the patio doors, and the lights in the sconces go on along the outside walls.

His mood changes again. He looks at her with an excited expression. "I may be able to hold objects from *La Alma Verde* in my hands and to get my ancestor's story historically documented."

"I hope so, Carlos. It really drives you, doesn't it?"

"You've been in my underground cave."

"I didn't get that close a look at everything. I couldn't figure out how to work your lights. I was using the storm lantern."

"I know, I smelled the smoke after you blew it out."

"I did see a lot of photographs of Ireland on the walls."

He shakes his head. "Most of those photographs are taken in Galicia."

"Really?" she asks.

He looks thoughtfully at her for a few moments, then says, "I remember driving for days through Spain. The afternoon heat was intense and it was so quiet except for the wind, which brought up the dust on the roads, and then you hit Galicia and find the terrain suddenly changed. You think you're in Ireland with the green, rolling landscape and the rain. You know you are in Spain only because your map tells you that you are, yet it feels like a place elusive of Spain. Resistant somehow to the rest of it. And it's through this Irish weather that you reach La Costa de Muerte, and the wildest, most unforgiving wind you'll ever experience."

He takes a drink of his wine. "The Celts invaded Galicia a thousand years before Christ, and the local instrument, the gaita, are bagpipes, similar to the Irish bagpipes."

"I didn't know," she says.

He nods. "Also in the sixteenth century, Irish lacemakers

settled in Galicia and taught the Spanish to make lace. Anyhow, Galicia reminds you of Ireland but it isn't Ireland. Ireland," he says, shaking his head, "is dreamy and cruel in its own way."

She feels as if he is describing a love affair. A trace of agony is on his face as if he is confounded by the nature of the place, by its imponderability.

He takes a map from his pocket folded to the southwest corner of Ireland. She sees Kerry and the western sea, the Blasket Sound. He has circled place names here as he had done on the map of Spain. She can read some of them: Glenbeigh, Clonee, Athea, Annascaul. The Irish place names not dusky and seductive like the Spanish ones, but headstrong and beguiling. Haunted sounding. Ballinskelligs, Cahersiveen, Bantry.

He has circled them as if he can lay claim to them, she thinks, and a flux of anger rises in her. She says suddenly, "People have silly notions of the Irish."

"Do they?" His eyes are fixed now to hers, trying to read them.

With an ironic tone she asks, "I know how you feel about the land, but what did you think of the people?"

He pauses and half smiles, knowing he is in a precarious place with her.

"They were thought of throughout Europe as an untamable people."

"Were they now?"

He looks at her with a hidden smile. "Freud said that the Irish were the only people on earth who could not be helped by psychoanalysis."

She breaks into a reluctant smile.

"They are lonely by nature," he says.

She tries to keep the smile on her face, but her heart is going hard, finding herself resentful of his romanticization.

He seems to see this in her face and quickly switches the focus of what he's saying: "I think the Irish are a people longing for adventure."

"It sounds to me like you're describing yourself."

Anything he might say right now could infuriate her.

"They were great warriors." He winks at her.

"Yes, in the time of Cuchulain," she says. "And what about now? Do you think they're fine little people dancing in green shoes?"

His face darkens.

"What you have," she says, "is a notion of Ireland."

Something in her tone has wounded him. She looks away at the glimmering wall sconces and feels regret for her harshness. He is leaving. Tomorrow night while she lies in her bed dreaming of Enrique Salazar, Carlos will probably be flying over the Atlantic. Pressing eastward he will experience a very short night and move through it as if it were only a pastiche of darkness. It should be her going to Ireland, she thinks, but she cannot even bring herself to telephone Noreen Feeney.

"I'm just jealous that you're going," she says by way of apology.

"Why did you leave Ireland?"

The question takes her off guard. "A lot of people leave . . ."

"Why did *you* leave?"

She stares at the candle flame moving back and forth in the votive. She breathes hard, then meets his eyes. He can see, she knows, that this question holds pain for her.

"How long will you be in Ireland?" she asks.

"It might be the entire summer. Possibly longer, depending on how the dive goes."

She nods and stares at the poplars, silhouettes now past the hacienda wall.

"So I'll fly out of Albuquerque tomorrow afternoon, then out of New York tomorrow night to Limerick."

"You make it sound so simple. To me it feels a world away."

He smiles. "You're right. It really is. We take traveling so much for granted in our time. It's so easy to travel a world away. But if you think of what it meant in Enrique Salazar's time . . . to make a pilgrimage to a holy shrine people set aside their lives. They crossed Europe to get to Santiago de Campostela, sleeping on roadsides half starved to death, always knowing there was a good chance they wouldn't make it. Wouldn't survive it. All because they wanted to look into the face of a certain martyr or touch a statue's hand. The medieval traveler knew that a passion is worth giving your life over to."

An indefinable chemistry floods Fiona's heart. She warms to him, and he seems to read it in her eyes.

He smiles, a blush infusing his skin. "I sometimes think I was born in the wrong time."

His smile is contagious. "I think maybe you were, too."

With great animation, he says, "I've always felt this vague longing for some older time. And when I first read Enrique Salazar's diary I knew some echo of that story in me already, like I'd always known it, or it was written in my blood. Do you know what I mean?"

She nods.

"But you can't hold a story in your hand. You can't feel its weight and contours. I guess that's why I love artifacts and relics. Restoring them gives me some satisfaction. History resides in objects. If I can find a coin or a piece of jewelry from *La Alma Verde,* some iron pipe or a knife. Something . . . I have a direct connection to my ancestor."

She wonders if this is true; if finding relics from the ship will even remotely soothe this passion in him.

"But you can't prove the part about the women," she says.

He looks at her thoughtfully. "But I can document that story. And it can be preserved and memorialized in the archives."

"I have a question," she says. "How did Enrique Salazar get back to Spain from Ireland?"

"Legends don't allow for such awkward questions." They both laugh. "He was just there again one day."

"It's a wonderful story. The story of your ancestor."

"There's something unfinished about it," he says.

"What do you mean?"

"There's a mystery to it I wish I could resolve."

"Some things are mysterious by nature," she says.

He considers her words a moment, then seems to dismiss them. He looks at her pointedly. "Who knows what I'll be able to uncover in that sea."

The way he says this frightens Fiona a little, as if he imagines he might locate the island of the three women; as if he has some wild dream of finding his way into the story itself.

But looking at him across the table, he looks so intelligent, so rooted in the real world, and her moment of fear strikes her as unfounded.

"Enrique Salazar must have been a beautiful man," she says.

He looks at her intensely, that palpable flurry of sympathy passing between them.

"It's captured my imagination," she says.

"I have photographs of Enrique Salazar's house in Galicia.

And I have more cards and photographs taken in Spain that you'll be certain were taken in Ireland."

He touches her hand where it lies on the table.

In her car, she follows Carlos's truck along the rough Tesuque road, its narrow ascents and descents. It is dark now, only an occasional streetlight among the old cottonwood trees. As they pull up to Carlos's small adobe house, set away from other houses, two horses in a corral are visible in the headlights. When both cars are off and the lights extinguished, she sees the creatures in silhouette. One of them neighs.

She steps down after Carlos into his front room as he switches on a lamp. Standing in his living room, she can see the entirety of the house. Doors open on two other rooms besides the kitchen. He goes into the small study, switching on another lamp. His desk is uncluttered, bereft-looking in comparison with the underground room he keeps in the antique store.

Through the other door she can see his bed, wide and unmade, a deep blue cover hanging half on, half off.

Once she'd thought his house would be full of antiques, but now seeing its easy bareness, the thought of clutter seems strange to her. A curved adobe fireplace in the corner issues the smell of burnt piñon, its floor black with ash. On top, a few unlit votive candles in red, smoke-stained glasses.

She notices a tan leather chair, well worn, an ottoman in front of it. Clearly he has sat many hours in this chair. She imagines him in repose here, thinking, daydreaming.

She is about to sit in it when he directs her instead to a Taos bench, just wide enough for the two of them. "So we can look together," he says.

He hands her a packet of pictures, and they sit. Windswept,

green landscapes in overcast light. It looks like the Doolough Valley, she thinks.

"Galicia," he says. "Northern Spain."

A postcard reads *Betazos*. "A Celtic village," he says. "Where Enrique Salazar lived." A particular house is circled, an ancient stone house with wrought-iron balconies on a narrow, ascending road closely crowded with similar houses.

Another depicts a town photographed from water near evening. It looks like a great balcony of light. The place seems to belong more to the sea than the stone cliffs and the mainland behind. "La Coruña," he says. "The port from which the Armada set sail."

She leafs through the images of estuaries, terraced slopes, women gathering shells at low tide, granite churches, and streets gleaming with rain.

He holds on to the photograph of Betazos. "He couldn't forget the time in Ireland. He could not forget the three women. He gave them Spanish names."

"What were they?"

"Caridad, Esperanza, and Inocencia."

"Charity, Hope, and Innocence."

"He wasn't originally Galician. But he moved to this town and to this particular house so he could always face north toward Ireland."

She looks through the pictures in the packet and finds one of a field with the sea visible just beyond it. She remembers cabbages so lushly ruffled and heavy they made dips in the earth. She remembers dancing with Michael, her mother clapping. The three of them giddy, breathless. Emotion, held so long in abeyance, rises in Fiona's chest. She looks at Carlos and away again.

"Where are you?" Carlos asks.

A few moments pass. She cannot answer him, her heart clamoring. He touches her hand. She wants to explain the emotion she feels.

"My mother died recently."

"I'm sorry, Fiona." He leans in close and puts his arm around her. A wave of tenderness for him moves through her in his arms. In spite of her grief, she is aroused by his closeness.

Something she barely senses, a pause in his heartbeat, a flux of confusion leaving his chest and coming into hers, makes her let go of him.

He is looking at her, not knowing what to say.

"You said you had a diary excerpt," she says.

He looks taken aback, and his hesitation tells her that he's protective of it. But after a few moments' consideration, something comes alive in his eyes and a tingle of excitement moves through her. He gets up and goes into his bedroom. She hears a drawer open and close. He comes back in, unscrolling a piece of paper as he sits down next to her.

He waits a moment, takes a breath, and then reads: *"It is when I reach the highest pitch of terror in my dreams that one or the other of the women comes and offers me her breast like I am a child."*

In his voice, Fiona detects a vague tremor of nerves or excitement which he struggles to suppress. But as he goes on, his voice warms and slows, finding its rhythm.

"They always come singly. Never together. And there is no order to who will come when. I know them now by touch and by the mood and tenor of their voices in the dark. I cannot keep the number of days and nights clear. The one I have come to think of as Caridad came to me once when I cried, and something happened. She sopped my sweat and spoke to me in her indecipherable language."

He stops a moment and looks at her, then continues, the

nervousness fully evaporated from his voice, a certainty in its softness. *"She climbed in bed beside me and gradually the comforting became something heated between two people."*

Fiona's heart quickens.

"Almost every night since, no matter which woman comes, the comforting becomes something more. I feel my strength again and during the day I am vigorous and restless and I walk outside in search of the women. But I can find not a soul anywhere the length and breadth of the island and this, the only cottage here.

"If I do not sleep and cry out in dreams, they do not come. Only when I am suffering, feverish. And then she is there, as hungry for me as I am for her, and soon I am inside her, feeling every nearly indetectable flutter and tensing of her muscles around me."

He waits a few moments before he rolls the paper back up, holding it scrolled in his hand. He does not look at her.

Fiona's heart beats high in her chest. She is afraid that he can hear it.

After a few moments he asks, "Do you speak Irish?"

She meets his eyes and smiles. "A little. We had it in school, but it's been a long time."

"Will you say something to me in Irish?"

She laughs softly, surprised by the delight she feels at his request. "Let me think." She struggles in her mind to translate a phrase from their earlier conversation, the thing he said about the Irish being untamable people. He watches her face, his eyes lit as she speaks. *"Ta´ mo mhuintir dos machtaithe,"* she says.

His smile broadens, almost as if he understands what she has just said. He lets go a little breath. "Will you say it again?" He waits with expectation.

She sits back from him, smiling. "Don't you want to know what it means?"

"No. Don't tell me what it means."

"Oh, but I want to tell you," she says excitedly, knowing he'll laugh.

"No, Fiona," he says quietly, firmly. "I don't want you to tell me." A softness is in his look as he holds her eyes.

She is sensing him out now, the heat of him warming the air between them, her Irishness a palpable source of eroticism for him. *"Ta´ mo mhuintir dos machtaithe,"* she says, more slowly this time, feeling the language in her mouth, elemental as waves slapping at a fortress of rock.

As she speaks he kisses her softly, tasting the words, making her pause between syllables. She feels herself opening to him, her blood softly rioting, and a thrill rushes through her when he touches her back. His hand moves up, grazing the nape of her neck, and he brings her face in closer to his. The kisses intensify and she is reclaiming the skelligs and western cliffs of Ireland. The beaches and the rocky points, all feel inseparable from her at this moment, her own contours softened by the same wind.

They break the kiss and look at each other. He moves a strand of her hair from her eyes and asks, "Will you stay with me tonight?" He is offering her what the women offered Enrique Salazar. A balm against suffering. She waits to answer and he kisses her again. She remembers that he is leaving tomorrow and her heart drums. She feels afraid that he may never come back.

He looks into her face expectantly. She is shaken, struggling to think. She wonders if he will be changed by his contact with the past. He runs headlong toward it while she, fearing its power, has for so long avoided it. Maybe she realizes more than he does the danger of inviting something so arcane into your life.

She thinks she will say no. That they should wait until he

comes back. But he takes her hand and turns it so it is palm up. He touches the skin at her wrist where her veins show, searching for her pulse. When he finds it, he bends down and presses his mouth to it.

Liquid warmth washes through her. She moves her other hand through his hair, parting it away from the back of his neck, unable to resist kissing him there.

"For so long," she says softly, close to his ear, "I've been living only at the surface of myself."

When he is inside her, Irish words float up of their own accord. She utters things she has not thought of for so long, language inspired by the rhythms of their bodies together. Urgent and patient, by turns.

Leim an bhradain, the salmon's leap, a phrase from a poem. *O'a mhaighdean rocheansa,* the beginning of a prayer.

As she moves toward rapture she remembers a canticle, *cleitearnach sciathan,* the flutter of wings, the words coming quick on her breath. She repeats them, each sound singeing the air.

While they lie in each other's arms, Carlos describes the Blasket Islands seen from the tiny Irish town of Coumenoole on a clear day, like the humps of whales in rough water. He tells her about a stone monument to the Spanish ships near a bed-and-breakfast where he stayed in Dunquin.

She tells him the things she misses: the prongs she used to toast bread over the fire, the smell of turf. The hens invading the kitchen on a summer's day.

They lie together all night in the dark, talking and making love.

*

At the edge of sleep, she whispers place names: Athlone, Roundstone, Doolough, Cashel Bay. They are soft green words. The
more she says them the more they harden into jewels. A necklace
strung together on her breath.

She dreams of the history nun at the school in Roundstone
asking her where she was born, and her answering, "Athlone."
And the nun saying to her, "Where the White Bull of Con-
naught was slaughtered by the Brown Bull of Ulster. Athlone.
Place of Entrails."

At dawn she dresses quietly. She wonders if she should kiss him,
wish him good luck on the excavation. But watching him
dream, she cannot bring herself to wake him. His heart is already
in Ireland, she thinks. He is already diving down into the
Atlantic looking for the remains of the past.

Smarting with the wrench of disengagement, she drives
home before the sun is up in the sky.

PART TWO

THE REALM OF
FAERY

NINE

ROUNDSTONE,
COUNTY GALWAY,
IRELAND
1960

The March wind came to the cottage door that
morning, knocking it open, sending Fiona's patterns
into a flurry, the spools to the floor, leaving a general
tumult on the kitchen table where she'd thought
she'd created order. She could smell a storm brewing,
the sky lowering, dim for this time of morning. She
had four dresses to make, and all spring and summer
to make them. Three bridesmaid dresses, pink with
tulle skirts and layers of voile. And a white wedding

gown of "sleeping beauty satin," a languid fabric, slippery and difficult to seam.

Four dressforms stood in the sewing area facing into the kitchen, each adjusted to the figure of a different girl. Jane had always kept two there, but when Fiona had had two more delivered and had set them up, Jane had called them "the little crowd."

Ann Finley had told Fiona about a fashion school in Dublin. What she needed was experience, designing and making dresses. The headmistress of the school was looking for girls who could show photographs and examples of their own work.

The bride-to-be was Martha Hanrahan, not a girl Fiona particularly liked. But that didn't matter much. She'd only have to see her now and again for fittings. She'd already gotten Martha's measurements and listened to the worst of her excited blather. Martha'd asked that Fiona inset a lace bib from her own mother's wedding gown.

"It's my heirloom. A bride needs something from her own mother's wedding," Martha had said.

Judith Nolan, one of the bridesmaids, met Fiona's eye and looked away. It was on the air.

Fiona gazed unperturbed into Judith's face with what she thought of as her "hidden smile." She had cultivated the expression: a vague, ironic demeanor, as if she were thinking condescending thoughts. She'd never let the girl think she had any power over her.

Fiona had obtained the commission by telling Martha about the "sleeping beauty satin," something she'd discovered in the depths of the fabric store in Galway, a thick, milky fabric that poured off the bolt. It came in different colors that could be fashioned into rosettes for ornamentation or embroidered with seed pearls.

Martha had described the dress she imagined for herself and Fiona drew it. She'd do the entire commission for a song, she'd said. "Save your money, Martha, for other things a bride might need."

And now with everything in place and all her supplies collected, Fiona itched to get to work.

She was happy to have the house to herself, to concentrate fully. Jane had gone to spend three days in Galway with Noreen Feeney, who had a sister there. They did this together every now and then, making a party of it, visiting the dance halls at night.

Once when Jane was angry with Noreen she had confided to Fiona, "I draw the men to the table, and I refuse them. Now and then one of the ones I refuse will chat up Noreen."

"That's why she's your friend," Fiona had said to her.

That had hurt Jane a little. Jane spent a lot of time with Noreen. Her family owned a shop in town and Jane went in to help out a few days a week.

"Why don't you dance with any of those men?" Fiona had asked Jane.

"It's fate that we're here on this farm with our land bordering Ned McGinty's," Jane said. "Fate decrees that I'll marry that man. It's preordained. I've my heart set on him. I'll not flummox things by getting mixed up with another man."

"Well, why do you go to the dance halls then?"

"For something to do, for God's sake, so I don't climb the walls with the boredom!"

Fiona would begin with the pink triplet dresses, do them in unison; save the most delectable and difficult for last.

She was struggling with her plans and adjustments for the pattern when thunder sounded softly and the morning light went a shade dimmer. She heard a man humming outside and looked out the window, stunned to see Michael Devlin coming to the door wearing a dark green frieze coat. He nodded and smiled when he saw her.

"My uncle's not in his cottage below," he said. "Is he here?"

"No." Fiona paused a moment, then gestured him in.

He glanced at the dressworks and away and she wondered if he even remembered what he'd said to her that one other time he'd stood in this room. She cleared a spot at the table and pulled up a kitchen chair for him.

"Would you like a cup of tea?"

"Lovely." He nodded. The wind was quieter now. He gazed outside at something through the top half of the door, which she had kept open, and she wondered what and glanced out herself but saw nothing out of the ordinary. He was pensive, different in manner than she remembered him to be, reticent even in the way he took the beaker of tea.

She stood near the stove looking at him, and when he remained quiet, she said, "I'll just go on with my work then."

"Yes. Go on."

She struggled to concentrate for a few minutes, attempting to adjust the measurements and redraw the outline of the pattern to Judith Nolan's figure. The day went sullen outside and the rain began. She looked up at Michael. He sat facing out, still wearing his frieze coat, listening to the drops. She realized in the beat of a moment that he was sensing her out, aware of her.

"I might be planting your fields," he said, breaking the silence. "My cousin Eamon and myself."

"Really?" Fiona knew Mr. Ryan had been in pain all winter with his rheumatism.

"He might not let me do it. You know the way with him. He's stubborn. But my mother doesn't want him doing it. He's suffering murder with the joints."

Michael got up and paced about, then finally said, "I'll just have a look, shall I?" Ignoring the rain, he walked out, eyeing the hill from different directions. Once he bent down over the plowed ground and took some soil between his fingers and smelled it.

He tossed his long hair from his eyes like a horse. Since that day he'd stood in her kitchen, she'd turned him into a million animals: horses and donkeys and rams and dogs and swine. She'd seen him in every animal foraging in fields and tillage, and the wilder sort, the foxes and the hares. She looked always into an animal's eyes, some seeming to her more human than others as if under spells of enchantment. She heard an animal in the trees once and decided it was a stag with twelve-point antlers. An Irish deer, the large, extinct sort. That would be the creature Michael might be, she thought, a low belling sound to its voice; a sound full of sex and darkness.

When he came back in, he paced a little and his eyes passed over her and away.

"You don't remember what you said to me once, do you? The other time you were here?"

"I do, of course," he said. "Circe and the alder trees."

She stood before him, feeling a thrill of boldness come into her. "Circe turned men into animals."

He took her in now fully and smiled, a beautiful tension all around his mouth as if he were trying not to smile, trying to hold it back. And then it deepened as if he were eating something both sweet and tart and holding the flavor in his mouth. Dimples appeared and a rise of color on his skin.

"Ah, here he is," Michael said, his eyes leaving hers suddenly. Mr. Ryan was scaling the hill.

"We'll see now who wins this battle," Michael said, and went out to meet him.

Fiona watched. Michael was taking his time with things, blathering on, talking planting with him, perusing the field.

She'd not learn the outcome because they walked together down to Mr. Ryan's cottage and disappeared inside. Later when she'd found a rhythm to her work, she heard footsteps, got up, and saw him leaving, passing under the alders and disappearing up the road.

That evening Fiona walked far into the field across the road, a long way over the undulations of what was left of a path overrun now in dock and nettle, past the faery fort, and stood over the miry water, still as a mirror. She turned a circle with her eyes closed and, opening them, suddenly imagined she saw, for the fraction of a moment, Michael's image imprinted on the air across the pond. She remembered Jane growing into a frenzy, repeating this circle again and again, her arms around herself, head back in longing for Ronan Keane. Fiona told herself she had not come here for this. She'd just wanted the freshness of the air. She'd not be like Jane staying long at this. She'd take the single sign and not ask for a hundred. She was not like her mother, and her spells and incantations would not be weak as water because they would not be cast in neediness. They would be little commands to the elements. Hers would come true, she said, looking defiantly at herself in the placidness of the lake, the dark beginning behind her in the trees.

And she was right. Early the next morning, Michael Devlin returned.

Michael and his cousin Eamon walked the perimeters of the fields.

Now and again Fiona looked out at them through the window, watching them pitch stones from the plowed ground, throwing them to the sidelines. With his sleeves rolled up mid-biceps, Michael dug his arms into the ground, pulling up spiky bits, black branch and roots. Once when she opened the door, she heard Eamon say, "Jayz, he missed a lot. We'll plow it again."

"He's old now," Michael mumbled.

Birds wheeled above them, settling sometimes, picking at the unearthed weeds.

Eamon was quiet, watchful eyes peering out from under sandy-colored hair. Only when she got a good look at his face could she see they were cousins, from the bones of their faces, the flirtatious gleam in the eye. Eamon caught her once looking out the window at them and called Michael's attention to her and the two smiled. She retreated, miffed when she heard them laughing.

She fed them both a big meal that night. Fried eggs and rashers and potatoes mixed with onion and cabbage. Brown bread.

"Will ye come to Doolough for Beltane, Fiona?" Eamon asked, that teasing look to him.

"Beltane?" she asked.

"Bel's fire," Eamon said. "The May fires. It's the best festivity of the year."

"It's a very old custom, the bringing in of summer," Michael said. "Cattle brought down from winter pastures are driven between two sacred fires. Men and women dance and leap the flames."

"And make free with one another," Eamon said, and winked at her. She looked away from him.

"Yes." Michael smiled. "And we all drink from the cauldron of inspiration."

"What do you mean by that?" Fiona asked.

"You'll have to come and find out for yourself," Michael said. "We're all inspired by euphoria on that day."

It was lashing rain late the next afternoon when Jane came back from Galway. Eamon had gone to the pub and Michael was sitting in the kitchen eating the rashers that Fiona was frying.

"Mother, this is Mr. Ryan's nephew Michael. He and his cousin started putting in the crops yesterday."

He stood noisily, almost knocking down his chair, swallowing his mouthful. "Hello, missus," he said, reaching his hand out to her. "Michael Devlin."

She paused before taking his hand, her eye fixed uneasily to him. "Where's Mr. Ryan?"

"The rheumatism. He's resting his joints in my mother's house in Doolough."

"Oh, well then," Jane said, and stepped farther into the room, drinking Michael with suspicious eyes, looking around her at the dishes and the empty tins. "Are you staying in his cottage below?"

"I am."

"And your cousin as well?"

"He's here only a few days more. Just until we finish seeding." Michael looked at Fiona and smiled. "I'll stay on for the season and help you out with running things."

"You ought to get down to the cottage so you can get an early start in the morning," Jane said.

"I just gave him a fresh cup of tea," Fiona said.

Jane peered at Michael. A tense silence held the air.

"All right, then," Michael said suddenly, congenially. "I'll get early to bed."

"And you know, Michael, once the crops are all in in a few days, there's loads of work to do around here. The chicken house needs to be cleaned out."

There was a pause.

"In fact, it could do with a lick of paint."

"All right, then," he said. "Thank you for the meal, Fiona." He smiled at her and she felt a thrilling little stab in her gut.

"Cheeky of him asking you to cook for him," Jane said once he was out.

"He didn't ask. I offered!" Fiona said, watching her. "So what's wrong? Why on earth don't you like him?"

Jane took a deep breath, struggling with her thoughts. "He can buy his own food like Mr. Ryan did."

Fiona turned from her and began clearing Michael's dishes from the table, but Jane moved in for the frying pan, clucking her tongue at the grease. She put it under the faucet, filling it with fairy liquid, and scrubbed as if it were a great irritation to her. They heard a ruckus in the yard and stepped out to see Michael descending the hill in the rain, moving not toward the cottage but toward the fence between their property and McGintys', where Oonagh, Jane's favorite cow, had knocked down two planks of the fence and trespassed into Mrs. McGinty's new planted garden.

Michael sloshed through the mud after her in his Welling-
tons, taking the situation in hand with Ned McGinty, who had
stepped out into his yard at the noise. Michael slapped the cow
on the rump and drove her back through the fence, gesticulating
in a friendly manner to McGinty.

"A diplomat, he is," Fiona said.

Jane waved at Ned and gestured for him to come over. He
looked at her a beat before lifting his forearm and dropping it.
Fiona could sense the dark reef settling on her mother's heart.
When Michael was back again and the cow contained, he took
hammer and nails to the fence, and when it was repaired, Jane
waved him up to the house.

He came in bringing the mud with him. Jane gave him a
glass of whiskey and took one herself.

"Thank you for that, Michael," Jane said. "About the cow,
that'll not be a problem when the fences come down between our
two properties." Fiona's heart went quick with embarrassment.

"You see, Ned McGinty and I will eventually marry."

Michael drank silently and gave a polite nod.

"Ned wouldn't care a fig if both cows trespassed and if my
chickens roosted in his roof. He'd not care," Jane said, stressing
the words. "It's his old bitch of a mother is the thorn in both our
sides."

Michael looked past Jane's shoulder at the photograph of
her at sixteen standing on the beach, gazing from Jane to the picture and back again, registering something, a softness coming
into his expression.

"But my cow Oonagh is a canny girl. More like a donkey
she is with the brain in her. You see, she's put her eye on a certain
black bullock of Ned's. When you hear her bawling, it's for that
bullock who she's gotten the sniff of on the air."

Michael listened with a little smile, seeming in wonderment over what she said, gleaning it to the full. Jane's eyes flitted to his face and away, intrigued by his response to her. She suppressed a smile.

"A canny girl, that cow," Jane said, nodding her head as if she and the cow were in collusion with one another.

Those early days with the ground just seeded, Fiona watched Michael from behind the kitchen curtain. He was always engaged with the planted mounds, bent over them as if in a dialogue with the hidden seeds, his dungarees pewtered at the knees and down the front of the calves from all the kneeling.

He was an elemental, she thought. Like the Green Man from fairy tales who dressed in leaves and had sprung from the trees themselves. Michael, with the shimmer of soil on his hands and clothes, seemed to have sprung out of the ground. To be one with it.

Sometimes he stood outside with his arms crossed as if he were waiting for the seeds to sprout. Once she saw him staring far off at the horizon, and she ached to know what his thoughts were, and what it was exactly that he thought of her.

When he came in for tea, he was windblown and smelled of the field, ruddy from his attentions to it. She stood behind him while he ate and secretly studied his hair. After a high wind it looked thick and flossy, a mass of black lamb's wool. She imagined washing it, weaving soap through the thick, dark waves.

She took four yards of fabric outside to wash under the outdoor pump. She could feel his eyes on her as she bent over the tub, the lather dripping from her wrists and forearms and onto her dress. She rinsed the fabric carefully, never casting a glance at him.

As she pegged it up on the line, he sang, "The winds are wild around Drumore Castle . . . ," and she pretended not to hear.

An envelope came from Ronan Keane. Photographs of dry tributaries and ditches. Red cliffs under intensely blue skies. A photograph of a sunflower taller than the dark-skinned woman standing beside it, its head huge and lolling, the woman's head small in comparison, her black hair blowing out to one side.

Fiona could not summon her usual curiosity for the pictures or concentrate much on the letter, her heart so much in Roundstone, in the small acres of dark, new field.

It was a Friday evening, Jane gone to the Moon and the Stars. Fiona was bent over the table, getting the cloth ready to cut, when Michael came in and sat down. He watched her working and she struggled to concentrate, to behave as if his presence were not a distraction.

He tugged on the fabric she was working, displacing it. She glared at him, trying to hide a smile.

"Don't touch it!" she hissed.

He touched it again and she pulled it away playfully. She gave him a bold, self-assured look, then smoothed the fabric back in place.

She sensed him wanting something from her, trying to begin a conversation. "The candle's gone out in front of your woman," he said, pointing at the Blessed Virgin Mary.

"My mother and her little shrines!" Fiona clucked her tongue. "Her endless devotions that Ned McGinty will propose marriage to her."

"No point to marriage," Michael said, and Fiona looked curiously at him. "Love's a changing thing."

She was stirred by his irreverence and by the way his eyes shone when he looked at her.

"You sound like a religious man, Michael," she said teasingly.

"Nah. I take my cues from nature."

"What do you mean?"

"The fields are my church. In the spring I plant. At summer's end, I reap. And then comes the dark of the year. That's when I think deep thoughts."

She restrained a smile. "And so where does this Beltane festival fit into all of this?"

"Ah, Beltane. Well, it's odd you mention it. I was thinking you might make a good Goddess of the Spring." He sat back and crossed his arms, looking her up and down.

"Goddess? Are you talking about the Greeks again?"

He shook his head dismissively. "I'll tell you the problem with the Greeks. Afraid of their goddesses. Odysseus was afraid of Circe. Now, an Irish hero was never afraid of a woman's power, but drawn to it instead. The Irish hero would have said to Circe, 'Put me between your sheets, Goddess, and turn me into the animal that I am.'"

She broke into an amazed laugh.

"Beltane is brilliant, Fiona. It's a celebration of the crops; of the sun and the moon. A young woman is selected to represent the Virgin Spring, and she enacts the fertility rite with the young man who represents the Sun God."

She met his eyes and looked away, setting another pin. "You mean they . . . ?"

He nodded his head emphatically, smiling.

A thrill rushed her at the way his voice softened when he said, "Excess is not only encouraged on Beltane, it's positively recommended!"

"And what is the cauldron you talked about?"

"A sip of the euphoric drink. The cauldron of inspiration. You'll find that out when you come. So will you come with me to Doolough for Beltane, Fiona?"

"Christ! My mother'd never let me go to anything like that!"

"It'd do your mother good to go herself."

Fiona cut carefully, and for a few minutes as she concentrated, he didn't interrupt her. She sensed him struggling with something in his thoughts, and when she put the scissors down, he said, "There's a ritual that precedes Beltane, Fiona."

"And what is that?"

"The young woman who would be the May Queen walks every night through the rows of new planted grain and her consort follows after holding a torch."

"And what does that do?"

"It insures the lushness of the field." He paused, then asked her with a smile, "Would you do me a service?"

She looked at him curiously.

"Would you walk now through the barley rows with your hair down around your shoulders, the way it is now?"

"What?" She laughed.

"You want the barley to come in lush, don't you?"

"Ah, no. You're mad."

"I'm not! Come on now and indulge me and you'll have a crop to be proud of." He took her arm, pulling her along.

"I'll put my shoes on first."

"No. As you are. I'll bring the lamp behind you and light your way."

They walked out into the dark, the ground cold under her feet. The air smelled of the deep of summer, though it was not yet April, and the stars were out in full. Fiona turned and smiled self-consciously at Michael. "All right then," she said. "I'll play."

As she walked up and down the rows, she laughed, but found herself liking the feeling of the air on her, the way it moved her dress about and the power the game gave to her, Michael following in her wake. As she quickened her pace to a canter, she felt an insolent delight.

When she finally came to a stop, having repeated her passage seven or eight times, she leaned against the wall of the house breathing deeply, drinking in the night air. Michael sauntered toward her with a smile, his eyes full of regard. "You are the May Queen," he said. "Look at you with your hair the color of fire."

She remained a few moments where she was, catching her breath and reveling in his attention before saying good-night.

Gazing into the mirror, her heart was going, her skin flooded with color and her hair wild and unkempt, redder than she'd remembered. She lit a candle and decided that her own hair was more brilliant than her mother's tame little flags to the Virgin. Everything about her was vivid. Even her freckles, which had always caused her dismay, seemed now exotic, like the bespattered petals of an orange lily.

She was still breathing hard, feeling too alive to try to sleep, so she went to the dressworks. Even the newly cut pieces of fabric looked pinker than they had earlier. She was full of elec-

tricity and the fabric shocked her when she touched it, three little sparks that moved from her fingers up her forearm and made
the ends of her hair staticky.

The next morning Fiona brought a cup of tea out to Michael in
the field. They were standing together smiling at one another,
Fiona waiting on the cup to take back up with her, when she
noticed Jane watching them through the kitchen window.

When she went back in, Jane fussed a bit, picking things
up and putting them down.

"Are you and Michael becoming good friends, then?" Jane
asked.

Fiona gave her mother a defiant look, refusing to answer.

When Michael came up later for the meal, Jane reminded
him in a clipping voice that the cottage below had a paraffin
cooker, even as she ladled his dish full of stew.

That night, finding one of his dirty shirts in the laundry
basket, she railed, "The cheek of him!" But she ended up washing it anyhow and pegging it up on the line outside where it
filled with air, stirring this way and that between slips and
knickers and aprons.

Jane's mistrust inspired rebellion in Fiona, and she couldn't wait
to meet Michael again in the field. Within days she had all the
pieces for the three bridesmaids' dresses cut and basted to the
forms. On the third night she breathed a sigh when she saw Jane
pour a second glass of whiskey, because she knew there'd be a
third, and after three, unless she had company, Jane could not
stay awake.

When Jane was asleep, Fiona went outside and found
Michael standing in the dark field, the lamp at his feet and

turned down low. Without a word she began to track her path through the rows and he followed. She lifted her chest, her heart seeming to lead her, everything that held and constricted her falling away: Jane's watchful eyes, litanies of oppressive words from the nuns, winks and innuendos from the girls at school and from Jane's friends. All of it streaming away. She quickened her pace, laughing softly, Michael's steps behind hers, and the light from his lamp cast her own shadow ahead of her, a black and urgent form. It had rained and the ruts of the field were full of rushing water, splashing at their shins and ankles.

Fiona didn't want to go back inside, and they walked together very late toward the bog and up a steep cliff overlooking the sea, watching the tides overlap one another, faint incursions of light moving along their edges.

The next morning when Fiona got out of bed and walked into the kitchen, Jane stared at the hem of her nightgown. Fiona looked down and saw that it was caked with dried mud. She met her mother's eyes.

"What were you doing last night?" Jane asked in a single breath.

When Fiona did not answer, Jane said, "Oh, God. What are the two of you up to?"

They heard the bell for the cream lorry at the bottom of the hill and, running to the window, saw Michael just coming out of his cottage, hurriedly buttoning his shirt. He hadn't gotten up early enough to do the milking.

Jane stepped outside, gesturing at him, and screamed, "That's another day before I can collect any money on the milk. I hope you're good at starching sheets, Michael, because you'll soon have me taking in laundry."

"I'm sorry, missus," he called out.

"Ye'll stop making yourself at home in this house alto-gether, Michael!" Jane screamed. "Ye can cook from now on in your own cottage! And I want you to stay clear away from Fiona! Clear away from her! I know a blackguard when I see one!"

Fiona turned a wild circle behind her and screamed, "Stop it!"

Jane slammed the door and turned in a rage on Fiona.

"I'm not having that one take advantage of you, for the love of Christ!" Jane cried. "I can spot a rake when I see one. He's looking to try and get a leg over you, Fiona!" Jane paused, a dark thought coming to her. "If he hasn't already!"

Fiona looked into her face, breathing hard, her hands in fists. "Maybe he has and maybe he hasn't!"

Jane grabbed her cup from the sideboard and smashed it to the floor. She covered her face with her hands.

After a long pause she said, "Fiona, don't give yourself and your heart so easily. There's something of the rogue about Michael. He'd leave you saddled with a child and disappear him-self to the four winds."

"I ruined your life, then. Didn't I?"

"No, no, Fiona. It's not what I'm saying."

"If you hadn't had me, you'd have gotten over your wild intrigue with my father, the rogue, and you'd be married now to your beloved Ned McGinty, wouldn't you?"

Jane was still, watching Fiona. "Hold on to your virginity, Fiona. It'll be a great asset to you."

For three days Jane did not leave the premises and Michael stayed clear of the house. He was up each morning early milking the cows, on time for the cream lorry. He cleaned the chicken house and repaired a broken door on the dairy.

On the third night Fiona fell into an agitated sleep and dreamed that her mother's hidden dress was standing at the foot of her bed, a stench coming from it. She got up and stood behind the dress, pulling at a thick, overly wrought seam along its back, a kind of spine that came loose of the dress, filleting one seam from another, the cord of stitches between prolific as fish bones.

She startled awake and lay there sweating, her breathing hot, feeling an almost ecstatic hatred for her mother. She tried to find relief in remembering the way she'd looked in the mirror after her first traipse in the barley. She loved her red hair now with a fierceness, because it marked her as different from Jane and because Michael admired it.

When she heard Jane's breathing change and she knew she was dead to the world, she got out of bed and, as she crept from the room, felt that exultant pull in her chest, thought of how her own power would precede her in the field. Fiona was sick to death of wishes and desires pulling at the air and everything remaining elusive. Sick of men as nothing more than ghosts. She wanted the solidity of the world as she moved through the dark kitchen, her heart banging at her chest. She hated ether, moods, and sorrow carried on air. She hated boredom and remorse. The tedium her mother lived in. She grit her molars together.

Not Michael's ghost but his body, the feel of his bones, the contours of him. She could make out the outline of him there waiting on her. His presence. His eyes were already accustomed to the dark and she could feel them on her.

So that night as he followed her brisk run through the aisles of the field, she turned suddenly and took the lamp from him and put it on the earth. She placed his hands on her waist, then slid her arms around his neck, pulling him after her onto the ground.

She drew his hand up under her nightgown, and he moved the undergarment aside until the gentle movement of his fingers in her slickness seared her.

He brought his fingers to his mouth. "Three tastes," he said. "Three tastes from the cauldron of inspiration." And then he put his fingers to her own mouth. Shocked, she let go a strange laugh, then yielded, tasting her tart saltiness on his fingers. The hours of unmitigated kissing went on, and the caress of his fingers in the secret heat of her.

The clouds moved across the night sky, and it seemed to her that the moon was swimming through them.

The next morning, though the three bridesmaid gowns were still unfinished on their forms, Fiona could not resist reaching for the sleeping beauty satin, the fabric plump and moist and unblemished. She found a tinge of pink, barely detectable in the morning light, in the flesh of the fabric. Irish skin never yet exposed to sun. She touched it gingerly as if she were touching Michael's stomach and his navel, the tender skin around his hardened sex, which she'd grazed with her fingertips the night before in the field.

She bent over the satin, touching her mouth to it and heating it with her breath.

She started when Jane came in to put the kettle on. Fiona's body pulsed damply, secretly, under her clothes. She stroked the fabric covertly, in collusion with it. Jane put bread in the toaster.

Now and again as they'd lain together, he'd stopped kissing her to watch her expression as he'd touched her. Whenever the pleasure had intensified and she'd been on the verge of rapture, he'd stopped. And she'd moaned and struggled to make him continue, but he'd told her they must draw it out. At the right moment they'd quench the fire.

She tried to concentrate on the dress, but the memory was alive and like a bellows to the flames that licked her insides.

Fiona realized she'd lost her way with the stitches and had to withdraw a line of them, the order of her thoughts in dreamy confusion.

She stood up and stretched and sighed. Through the window the newly sprouted barley was trembling in the breeze.

Jane came in to her later in the day.

"Can I trust you if I go out? I have to go to Feeney's."

"Yes," Fiona said, but could not hide the irritation in her voice.

Jane stewed about the room, then went out to Michael and set him to a task. She wanted the gate repaired before she came home. She made a big show that she was coming home in an hour, and Fiona knew it was a lie, just a ruse to keep her and Michael on their toes. She'd likely be much longer.

Jane wasn't gone ten minutes when Michael appeared at the door and then came in. "And which bridesmaid is this one for?" he asked, pointing to one of the presiding figures, then touching the bodice so the small, opalescent beads quivered.

"Judith Nolan."

"The one with the braids in her hair?"

"Yes."

"Simpering creature. This puts her to shame."

She felt herself shaking as he knelt slowly down before her and took one of her bare feet in his hands. He kissed the instep, then his tongue traveled up the back of her leg to the soft skin behind her knee.

"I'm afraid my mother'll come back," she said.

He pulled her legs forward in the chair, pulling her underwear off, then softly biting her inner thighs, causing her to jump and arch her back until his tongue found the center of her, where it stayed, swaying firmly like an underwater plant. Michael was on his knees in adoration, her hands in his hair and the voile skirts of the dresses rioting behind him, grazing his back in the breeze from the open door.

When he sensed her excitement reaching a pitch, he withdrew from her, pulling her dress down over her knees.

"No, Michael. Don't stop."

"Let's sustain it, Fiona."

"But I don't want you to stop," she said, on the verge of tears.

As he tried to withdraw, she grabbed his hands.

"You hear the gate out there? I've got to oil the hinges or she'll yell at me."

"If not for that, for something else," Fiona said, trying to hold him as he backed up from her, smiling.

Through the month of April as the crops sprouted they met on Friday nights or whenever Jane disappeared or fell into a whiskey-induced slumber.

Michael asked her to chart the days of her menstrual cycle, looking for safe times. One of her three safe days fell on Beltane. He told her that she would be the May Queen for the festival and stressed to her how important it was that they not have intercourse until that night. He tried also to keep her always on the verge of rapture, though he came himself sometimes in the field and rubbed the semen into a furrow of earth as if it were a woman's body.

Late one afternoon Fiona went to the hens to bring up some eggs. As she was picking one out from under the warm body of a pullet, Michael came in to her suddenly, startling her so Fiona dropped the egg, sending the hens into a stir. He lavished her with kisses. She could feel the hardness of him under his clothes. He was so on fire, kissing her face and neck, his hands up under her dress, she thought it would happen, that he'd forgotten about Beltane. Then they heard Jane's voice calling Fiona from the door of the house.

"Christ!" Fiona said in a fluster, brushing the feathers and floss of the hens from her hair and clothes, and with a shaking hand found three eggs in the straw.

Michael remained there hiding. She went up, still feeling the heat of him around her.

"What took you so long?" Jane asked.

"I was getting the eggs."

"Where's Michael?" Jane asked, peering out the door.

"I don't know." Fiona put the eggs on the counter and went straight to the refuge of her sewing.

Jane watched her for a few moments, sensing something, then went to the dishes and began to wash them.

Fiona faced away, feeling on the very verge of herself, every pulse in her going. She bent close to her sewing, her forearm brushing inadvertently at the silk, causing flushes of sexual pleasure.

The sighing of thread drawn through silk reminded her of Michael's breathing and caused her lust to flurry. She felt him with her still, the pressure of him against her so the rapture seized her, drumming through her. She bent her head and covered her face with her hand so Jane wouldn't know. She stifled her voice, but could hear within herself little ribboning cries.

She thought how exquisitely strange it had been. Like being at a great height, carried along on eddying air, pulled one way hard and then released. Then pulled again. Air with a sureness and strength to carry one and finally descend with one.

It had all passed undetected, and for a few moments she gloated that she had pulled the wool over Jane's eyes. She turned and watched her rinsing the glasses and felt herself reluctantly softening to her, feeling pity for her, worked down as she was by anticipation, promises never come to fruition. Jane making a terrible, reckless fool of herself for an oaf of a man.

That night Fiona didn't sleep. She left her work on the dresses around 3 A.M. and went down to Michael's cottage and, with a dim lamp, watched him sleep. She wanted to keep looking at him, to have him where she could see him, reassure herself.

That he was here, not a thought or a memory, but present in her everyday life, told her that her existence would not be like her mother's. She knelt on the floor close to him and studied his expression in sleep. Wistful, compliant.

She turned off his alarm, adjusted his blanket, and went out herself to milk the cows.

TEN

When she got out of bed on the first morning of May, Jane had already left to help out at Feeney's. Fiona pushed the curtain aside and the sun poured into the room, light segmented by the frames of the window igniting and warming the walls.

She hadn't said a word to Jane. She had tried to come up with an excuse about where she was going and in the end could think of nothing that would not make Jane suspicious and was afraid of foiling things.

The safest way was to just disappear with Michael and face the consequences the next day.

She washed and dressed and busied herself with final details on the three bridesmaids, snipping at loose threads and bits of net, pruning the hems of the tulle like hedges.

At ten o'clock she ran down the hill to meet Michael, who had borrowed his family's car. As they drove along the Galway road, slews of gulls flew over them, letting loose raucous cries and squeals.

The wind, sweet and brackish smelling, gusted through the car window. Now and then as they made the twenty-minute journey, he'd squeeze her hand or her thigh or lean toward her and kiss her.

She'd been imagining Beltane now for a long time, the pageantry and the dancing. And Doolough, a great open plain; firelight everywhere.

But the place they came to at last was not hill or dale or lambent meadow, but a winding road into a dark wood, which gave way to an old, rutted passageway. Branches scratched at the windows and the roof, and the car rocked in the shadows before reaching a clearing and an old thatched house under yew trees, the earth around it so loamy the house appeared to have sunk slightly. When they got out of the car, Fiona could see that the old cottage had many extensions, as if rooms had been added over time.

No one was inside, yet the kitchen was alive with habitation, lamps glowing at this early hour because of the dense shade of the yew trees. Dark logs supported low, whitewashed ceilings. Baskets filled with dried herbs and flowers hung from hooks. In the corner in a big limestone grate, embers dwindled to ash.

Their footsteps caused the floors and sideboards to creak. On a black dresser a basin and ewer rattled.

"I'll be leaving you here with my sister, Moira. She'll get you ready."

"But I want to stay with you," Fiona said, surprised.

"They have to get you ready. And they'll bring you to me when the sun goes down." He moved close to her, smiling, and touched the side of her face.

"But it's a long time before the sun goes down."

"Don't worry, Fiona. This is the way it works."

She looked uneasily around. "What things will they do . . . to get me ready?"

"Just relax you. Pamper you."

"But I don't know them."

"It's my sister and her friends, for God's sake." He laughed tenderly. "*I* know them and they'll treat you well."

She held on to his hands nervously.

"It could never be better between two people than the way it will be tonight. It binds us in a special way," he said in a soft, persuasive voice, holding her. "Okay?"

She nodded and pressed her face against his neck.

"Think of it this way, love. The bride has to be prepared to meet the bridegroom."

Female voices sounded outside.

"They're coming," he said. "Tonight we'll do what we've been waiting for so long to do." He gave her a smile that warmed her to the bone.

While Michael went out to meet them, Fiona remained within, peering out the window.

She spotted an august-looking woman with a long braid

down her back, light wheat-colored like Eamon's hair, and riddled with gray, coming through the trees. Fiona took her immediately for Michael's mother. A younger woman with dark hair who looked like Michael walked beside her. Following them, and still receded in the shadows of the trees, were two fair-haired, young women who could have been twins, linking each other, heads bowed, conferring. Michael greeted them and the five gathered a few yards from the house talking. They all turned at the same time to look at Fiona peering from the window. She dropped the curtain and went to the door but felt suddenly the shy violet and remained in the doorframe. They gazed quietly at her and she sensed their sussing her out. The importance of the role she would play pierced her. Michael's mother smiled and gave her a nod, then she and Michael departed together, going back through the woods.

Michael's sister and the two blond women approached the house.

"My brother tells me you're a bit nervous," Moira said, pulling a chair away from the table and gesturing for Fiona to sit. "But you've only got to relax. Everything is preordained."

The two blond women nodded and smiled at Fiona but did not speak. They moved ceremoniously to the stove and began preparing something.

Fiona only half listened as Moira chattered on a bit about the last time she was in Roundstone, about a girl she knew there who was also an acquaintance of Fiona's.

After a pause, Moira asked, "Do you understand the meaning of your role?"

"Yes, I think so. Michael said that . . . it's to ensure the lushness of the crops."

Moira leaned toward her. "You represent the Virgin Spring, untrammeled earth that will be seeded tonight by the god. Tonight you enact the fertility rite of the land. You and Michael will set the festival of pleasure into motion."

Though Fiona could see a trace of Michael in Moira's face, she could not warm to her.

"It may hurt you. Some women find the first time more painful than others do. When it hurts, relax all your muscles. Don't fight him or cry out."

It made Fiona uncomfortable that Moira spoke to her about such an intimate detail, and a sense of foreboding overcame her. Moira seemed to intuit it, a stern, formal look appearing a moment on her face and then passing. She nodded to one of the women, who brought Fiona a pewter cup with a milky drink concocted of herbs.

"Michael's filled with admiration for you, Fiona," Moira said.

Fiona closed her eyes and remembered his passionate words to her. She wanted to surrender, to trust that this was all right. There was more small talk, and Fiona guessed that it was to put her more at ease. About the fields Michael had planted. Questions about Fiona's dressmaking. She put the warm cupful to her lips, and found that she liked its sweet taste, strong with spirits. She drank, and it filled her with a dizzy, pleasant sensation, the bronze lamplight blurring around her.

The twins led her to a bath in a back room and helped take her clothes off. In a pleasant, tired state, she was helped into the tub and encouraged to lie back.

With slow hands the two women soaped and rinsed her skin, one of them humming in a low, tremulous voice.

They dried her and lay her on a bed in a dim back room

where the curtains were drawn; the room that had been
Michael's. She fell into a languid reverie. Hours may have passed
as she moved in and out of sleep. Now and then one of the
women would come in and massage her temples or her hands,
sometimes with oil, sometimes with water that smelled of laven-
der. She woke once thinking she heard mutinous winds rattling
the windows and doorjambs. But when she sat up and listened,
everything was silent.

Another cupful of the milky drink was brought in and she
took a few sips of it. The woman left it with her, and when she
was alone again, she gazed at the long birds like herons or cranes
on the dull green or gray wallpaper. As she lay back with her eyes
half-closed, the birds moved over the wall as they might move
through an overcast sky, passing upward, streaming up as if
thousands of them lived in the dark below the wainscotting.

She heard them screeching, wild, echoing screeches, by
turns grief-stricken and brazen, the ceiling above a hemisphere
into which they ascended. She brushed at the chintz bedspread as
if she were threshing through ferns, searching for Michael. The
birds' cries filled her with a terrible loneliness. They moved en
masse, a storm brewing, and the sky lowering, coming close to
her; a vague peal of thunder.

"Michael, Michael," she called. Gradually she realized she
was still in his room and could make out the door and the
armoire-like dark presences.

When it was time, the women dressed her in a loose, white gown
and wove flowers into her hair.

Walking on their way to the festival, Fiona was disoriented
with anticipation. Passing through gorges, flowering beds, and
broken stone facades, she veered off the path and was stung with

nettles. The two women guided her up to a plateau. She thought all the brightness before her was fire, but focusing her eyes, she saw women holding mirrors, angling them toward the descending sun, catching and for moments at a time containing its light. The pooling and glinting on the surfaces of the glass contributed to her elation and excruciating suspense, and she breathed strangely and made a little involuntary cry.

One of the women looked into her face, giving her an encouraging smile.

They faced an old ruin, a kind of stone oratory, its ceiling and two of its walls crumbled away. A rider appeared holding a torch. The horse neighed nervously and reared up, the man controlling the reins with one arm, holding fast.

The light in the mirrors began to change, a great momentum now to the sun's descent. It dimmed to crimson, burnishing the hips of the strutting horse. In a few moments the light went violet, then merged to twilight and incoming darkness. The women with the mirrors disappeared. The man on the horse put the torch to one bonfire and then to the next.

The air was rife with solemnity, the flames crackling now, an occasional wind hitting them that sounded like sheets beating on a clothesline. She sniffed the air for Michael, and the thought of him caused her heart to enlarge in her chest.

The two women led her to the stone oratory, firelit, and guided her to a kind of slanted stone bed, an altar low to the ground carpeted with grass and daisies and dandelions. They left her there lying on it, propped up on her elbows. Even the man with the horse was gone now, yet Fiona sensed people. She could smell them and, with the ends of her nerves, imagined she could hear them, but she could not see them.

The fire swelled, a preamble to Michael's coming. From the

dark patch of trees he appeared, walking purposefully toward her, wearing a white, voluminous robe, yet so light in weight that the breeze tousled it. Frail gold threads laced through the weave caught the firelight, as if it might submit to flame. When he bent over her, his skin and his eyes glowed as if he were bending over embers. The neckline of the robe hung so low she could see his body inside it, his dark nipples and his long, smooth loins, his cock at attention.

"*Cuileann agus coll,*"* he said, his voice reedy with excitement. She put her arms around his neck. She could see women now standing past the entrance portals, half-erased figures in the mist, and men gathered at the broken balustrade, monklike. Motionless. When she closed her eyes, she heard their collective breathing, amplified over the crackling of the fire, inspiring in her a wave of modesty and trepidation.

It seemed to her the firelight darkened. "What's wrong?" he asked her in an urgent whisper. She sniffled and shook but did not answer.

"It's all right," he said, pressing close to her. "*Trom agus carthen.*"*

She started as he pushed her dress up over her thighs, and her excitement crested at his knowing touch, the state of her like a ripe, dripping fruit. She reached for him and he struggled to enter her. Suddenly, the pain she felt was everything. She drew in a deep breath, remembering what Moira had said, and focused and softened her muscles. The only tension she allowed herself was at her forehead, a result of concentrating.

"*Agus fumseog gheal,*"* he panted. Every other muscle and

*holly and hazel
*elder and rowan
*and bright ash

nerve in her went malleable and he drove into her, holding his breath. The pain was gone and now the sensation overwhelmed all else, rending in its pleasure, prodding, bringing a shaft of light into her.

"*O bheal an atha,*"* he sighed.

She heard obsequious whispering and saw movement, light in her peripheral vision.

The more vigorous Michael grew, the louder the crowd became. Now the thought of the onlookers excited her, filling her with a kind of reckless lust. She pushed into him, met him each time. Like galloping, the momentum between them. Traveling, she felt they were on their way to some destination. She waited for him on the periphery of rapture and came when she felt him come.

Music played now, a reel on a pipe. Someone else pounded a bodhran.

They lay together panting. People threw hawthorn blossoms at them, Michael's forehead pressed to Fiona's shoulder as he recovered with closed eyes.

A shadow loomed near and Fiona saw a brown-haired girl standing over them, running her hand through Michael's hair. Fiona felt his awareness of the girl, though he did not open his eyes. She felt that he knew who was touching him. A throng of voices sent up revelrous cries, and the girl was gone.

Near the fire they joined the dancing, heads wagging as they moved, someone's hair brushing Fiona's face. The thud of feet on hard ground. Michael passed her in the dance again and again, his hand brushing her belly, trying to hold to her waist, but the momentum of the dance threw them wildly apart.

*from beside the ford

People were lively now, hectic; some kissed her as they swept past. She was breathless, confused, the night air heady with fire and sweat.

They were hit with a sudden onslaught of rain, people rejoicing in it. She lost Michael in the crowd. It seemed a while that she moved along through the festival, accepting hawthorn blossoms, sometimes being swept into a reel. She couldn't spot him anywhere in the crowd, so she went in search of him. She saw a moving shadow in the oratory and approached. Standing against one of the balustrades, she saw Michael kissing the brown-haired girl. For a few moments, the gravity of what she was witnessing did not register.

He looked beautiful, his eyes closed. They swayed slightly and seemed to be drinking and drawing at each other.

When she saw Michael tighten the embrace, Fiona breathed deeply, struggling to combat a rising anger, reminding herself that excess is recommended on Beltane.

She stumbled away, moving through the throng. The rain had stopped and couples writhed in the shadows, the air thickened with sex. She ran toward the outskirts of the firelight, a sudden gust of wind making her aware of tears on her face.

Over near the dark area of trees from which Michael had first emerged, Fiona saw Mrs. Devlin's matronly silhouette. She approached Fiona, studying her face with concern.

"It isn't right that the May Queen should be so out of spirit with the proceedings."

Breathing hard, Fiona did not speak.

"You should choose another partner now," Mrs. Devlin said.

"I can't," Fiona said.

"You can."

Against the enigma of Mrs. Devlin, Fiona felt insufficient. She had a piercing sense that Michael was part of something she could never find her way into. Heirlooms and history on a grand scale. Arcane secrets. There was a gravity to Mrs. Devlin, a shrewdness, an austerity as if she herself were centuries old, miraculously old as this vestige of forest.

She moved away from Mrs. Devlin and into the trees where she was free to weep.

She left on her own in the pall of night. Finding her way through winding paths, she felt ajar of herself and afraid of the magic of the place, imagining she might turn a corner and come upon herself crouched there weeping. She got to the Galway road and headed back in the direction of Roundstone.

Before dawn she stopped, finding an area of tall grass on the roadside. She lay down in it and wept, sinking into desolation as if it were the natural place for her, the truth of her that she had been resisting.

It was early in the morning when she scaled the hill to the blue color-washed house. When she saw Jane looking out through the kitchen window, she took a deep breath, ready to face her fury.

But opening the door, she found Jane sitting at the table. She looked distressed, exhausted, and would not meet Fiona's eyes.

"Are you all right?" Jane asked.

"Yes," Fiona said.

Jane sorted through a packet of Austrian crystal embellishments.

Fiona paused before her and, met with a long silence, went

to the faucet for a drink of water. She was about to leave the room when Jane said her name.

Fiona stopped and turned.

"Ye'll want to be careful, if you're . . . if you're on intimate terms with Michael."

"I am careful. I charted my days of fertility."

Jane winced, Fiona's words confirming what she'd suspected.

Getting up, Jane brushed past Fiona and went in to the Giantess. Fiona followed her and stood in the doorway, watching her stitch one of the Austrian crystal ornaments into the scalloped, overblown layer, and felt an anguished throb of need for her.

She wanted to be small again, to be folded into Jane's arms. She was tired of feeling older than Jane, this stretching and shifting of the strings that held them together.

"Mother," Fiona said. "Will you tell me about you and my father?"

Jane looked beseechingly at her. "Why, Fiona?"

"I want to know . . . what was between the two of you. In the beginning."

"I don't want to be thinking about that man, Fiona."

"He's my father," Fiona said in a soft, exasperated voice.

Jane looked at her, then down at her own hands holding the needle. She was quiet a few moments, bringing the past back to her.

"I was walking on the beach. He was following me, this young man with a camera. Handsome and well dressed. Not like the local boys. He'd been to France, he told me, and to school in England, and he said there were no girls so exquisite as me there. That I was an Irish beauty. He called me Queen Maeve. And I ate up his blarney, dyin' be told such things. He photographed me for hours, following me on the headlands."

She paused, then said in an appeal to Fiona, "When he looked at me . . . God, those moments were like none other in my life. When he kissed me, I heard the warning voices of the nuns in my head, but they meant nothing. What Ronan made me feel, I didn't want to resist. He told me about Paris and about the bright little towns in the south of France. He made me feel the wideness of the world. Don't I know even now, Fiona, such moments will not come again in my life. I thought that day on the beach with Ronan was the beginning of my life. That each day that followed would be as torrid. As deeply lived."

She paused a few moments, gazing before her at the glimmering hems of the dress. "And that day, Fiona . . . that was the day you came to me."

"How long was it after that, before you saw him again?"

Jane looked at her needle, moving it back and forth in the light. "Almost five months," she said slowly. "But he helped me then. He took me to Athlone and set things up there. After you he was careful to prevent another . . . another child. But I wanted another child from him."

"Why?"

"To bind him to me further."

"I wasn't enough to bind him to you."

"That's not it, love," Jane said, and tried to touch her, but Fiona recoiled. Jane turned back to her dress and took up her needle without energy.

Fiona stared at her mother's profile, the nape of her neck, bare and smooth and curved. How had Jane borne it? Fiona wondered. Desire and the way it could plague one? How could it not have demented her?

She got up and moved toward Jane and, going down on her haunches beside her, touched the Austrian crystal embellishments.

"I love these," Fiona said, gazing into Jane's face. "More than all of your other decorations."

Jane looked at them searchingly a moment, then raised her eyes to Fiona and embraced her. In Jane's arms Fiona felt herself going back. Back before Michael. Before Ned. Back to just the two of them. Some quiet, shared darkness. Some noise of water and membrane.

For three days Michael did not come. Fiona and Jane fed the chickens and milked the cows, did the routine of chores ordinarily left to Michael. In spite of herself, Fiona started each time she heard the engine of a car or footsteps on the road below. She longed for him to come. She saw pity in Jane's eyes. Would her own life pass thus, slowly, desperately, and without event, casting spells and saying incantations to bring her love to her. Looking for omens in all ordinary things.

Fiona took refuge in the work on Martha Hanrahan's wedding dress, struggling to control the fabric's wild, intensely anxious nature. White sleeping beauty satin, alive as the milky bedsilk of the oyster. It palpitated under her fingertips, and Fiona was convinced it was capable of sweating.

She struggled to shape and pin and cut, but it resisted her, fled from her grasp like fronds of slippery plant-life, her heart burning to fix it and ground it. With tremendous effort and concentration she cut the ghost of it, the first vague shape of it, piercing it with pins, wishing the life might ribbon out of it and make it still.

*

It was in the evening of the third night while Jane was gone, having driven down to the shops, and Fiona had begun preparations on a meal, that Michael came back. She was setting forks onto napkins on the table when she froze, hearing footsteps coming to the house. She had her back to the door when it creaked open.

"Fiona, love," he said, the sound of his voice going through her like a wash. Her eyes went hot and her breath came quick. She had imagined once in a moment of terrible longing that if he came, she might convey herself into his arms, press her head into his chest, keeping it there. But she froze where she stood.

He approached, embracing her, and she put her arms cautiously around him, keeping her head lowered, ripples of memory going through her: a flash of firelight, the wild pageantry and the thrall of the crowd. Michael kissing the brown-haired girl. She felt the hurt in the very craw of her, yet desire for him drummed in her so the two things fought.

"I wish you hadn't left," he said.

She did not reply.

"Why did you leave, Fiona?"

Every instinct in her told her to keep silent about the girl. Speaking of her would conjure her between them, and Fiona did not want her here in Roundstone in the fields that were hers and Michael's alone.

She broke the embrace and shook her head. "I don't want to speak about it, Michael." He held her eyes and she sensed him careful of her. He wouldn't press. There was a stillness to him now as he stood before her, something subtly different about him that Fiona struggled to define. A calmness, a lack of hunger. The festival was over.

*

When Jane came, she chattered on to him as if there had never been a rift between them. She seemed oblivious of how she looked to him, her hair askew, serving him meat and potatoes, steam from the cooking making her face shiny. Her eyes were tired and there was no trace of haughtiness in her.

Halfway through the meal, Jane said, "Do you know any poems, Michael?"

"There's a Spanish one I have in my mind."

"But I don't know Spanish," Jane said. "Give it in English."

He looked at Jane.

> *Uneasy ocean,*
> *never at rest.*
> *Oyster out of which*
> *the pearl of Venus was born.*

Under the table, Michael leaned the weight of his thigh against Fiona's leg, but he continued to look at Jane.

> *Your swells rage and shudder,*
> *trying to catch at the sand.*

Jane kept her gaze to her plate as if afraid to move. There was a long quiet before she met his eyes.

Michael took up his fork and again began to eat.

*

A little bit later that night, after they had finished eating and were drinking a second cup of tea, Jane asked Michael to go to Ned McGinty. To talk to him, to see if he could make him come around again to her.

"Why, Jane?" Michael asked. "Why are you so hard set on that man?"

She pointed to the picture above the shrine. "I was like a yearling then, Michael. In spite of the nuns and everything else. I was spirited and haughty and without apology. Ned knew me so. He carries the memory of that girl alive inside him."

Michael listened thoughtfully and intently, his eyes resting on Jane's face.

She got up and went to the wall, taking the picture down and bringing it to him. "Wasn't I the creature, Michael?" she asked, standing at his shoulder.

They looked together at the image of the euphoric girl with the wind whipping lightly at her hair.

"You were, Jane," he said softly. "You surely were."

ELEVEN

Late the next afternoon, Fiona peeked her head out of the kitchen door and saw Michael below in McGinty's yard talking to him.

"He's gone over!" Fiona said to Jane.

"Go watch, Fiona! Here's a basket. Go collect some eggs."

Fiona walked slowly down to the henhouse, watching the two men. Michael stood unmoving and, with a lowered head, listening to Ned. McGinty pointed at something in his field. It went on awhile, the talking and the nodding, before Michael gestured his head in the direction of town and the two sauntered off together toward the road.

"They're off to the pub, I think," Fiona said when she was back in the kitchen. Jane clapped her hand to her chest.

"I'll make you a cup of tea," Fiona said.

Jane lit every candle before the Virgin's statue, whispering to it as she did, "Sweet Mother of God." Moisture glazed her face. She moved about the room letting out deep, troubled sighs, opening the old dresser drawers and looking at the spangles and beads, ribbons and thread. She touched things absently, stirred them about.

Finally she sat in the room brilliant with candles, keeping the cup close to her face as she drank, the steam from the liquid making her eyes mist up. Every time the wind wiggled the doorjamb, she started.

When he finally came in nearly two hours later, they both stood, almost knocking their chairs over.

"He'll come to tea," Michael said.

"Oh, Michael!" Jane proclaimed. "Aren't you the star!"

"When?" Fiona asked.

"Midsummer's Day."

"No sooner?" Fiona cried.

"Jayzus!" Michael said. "Be happy with that! The man's like cement. It was like pullin' the teeth out of a bloody horse!"

Jane prevailed upon him, taking his coat and bringing him to the table to sit. "Tell us what was said in the pub," she cried.

"I never got him into the pub. He gave me a tour of a patch of his land that he wants to rent out for grazing. And then I had a bit of a time getting him off the subject of an indoor pump that needs repair. Christ, if he said another word about the mechanics of that pump—"

"Come on!" Jane cried. "Tell us!"

"Jane, you were right when you said the old woman is the thorn in his side. She's a terrifying creature, sittin' there in state in the parlor!"

"Christ," Jane said softly.

"He's petrified of the old bitch."

"Did the word *marriage* come up at all?"

"I must have used the word fifty times. I told him you'd been waiting for years and he said, 'Rome wasn't built in a day!'"

Fiona let out an ironic laugh.

"If he comes to the tea, he knows that's what it indicates," Michael said.

"God, I'll prepare like crazy for it," Jane said, standing, her face ablaze.

"Mother," Fiona said with a growing sense of foreboding, knowing the altitudes Jane's excitement could reach.

"What?" Jane asked.

Fiona paused. "Don't blather about it to Noreen and Lucy!"

Jane narrowed her eyes. "I don't blather, Fiona!"

"I mean, those women do blather, so I'd keep quiet over all of this."

Jane dismissed her, putting all manner of questions to Michael. Upset, Fiona retreated back to work on her dress.

The next morning Jane was up early and said she was too excited to go to Feeney's, though she was expected there. She drank tea and moved restlessly about the room, before finally taking up with the mirror.

While Fiona gave full attention to seed-pearling the cuff of one sleeve, Jane eased dresses and slips on and off, garments from years past, admiring herself, hands in her hair or holding the folds of a skirt, moving it back and forth, creating a breeze. She dabbed her mouth with color. Lined her eyes.

Jane asked Fiona's opinion about a dress she was wearing. Fiona nodded dismissively and Jane snorted.

"I'm busy," Fiona said in defense. Tiring of the dresses, Jane decided to make a special meal. She pounded potatoes and started on a dough for a crust, but kept pausing from her tasks to give herself an intense look in the mirror. She whispered to her reflection, in secret intercourse with it. She paused and listened and answered, shaking her head, gasping quietly as if reacting to something provocative that had been said. The mirror served as both her double and her lover's eyes.

In Fiona's peripheral vision, Jane and her reflection seemed always to be moving, trembling, shifting, while Fiona was searching for a still place in herself. She felt as if she'd returned from a trance, remembering with awe and shame how she'd surged and boldered. It hurt to remember her dementia, the way she'd willingly exhibited herself. But the knot that grew in her was that she'd allowed her passion to be made use of. And the brown-haired girl moved like liquid through her thoughts until Fiona was so close to the brown hair that she was looking through it like a curtain and it colored her moods so she saw the fabric and thread before her darkly as if through strong tea.

Michael came in for a glass of water. He stood before her looking to register her mood, her attitude toward him. In this moment she felt permeable, defenseless, so she cowered from him, afraid that he'd touch her, afraid of the charge that might rush into her from him.

She would not look at him.

He seemed to wait for an explanation but she would not mention the brown-haired girl. "I'm behind with my work," she said.

"You have until August to finish it. It seems to me you're way ahead of yourself."

She said nothing, but bent over the fabric, concentrating on drawing through a single seed pearl. His shadow hesitated there awhile before vanishing. The door opened and she heard his footsteps go down the hill.

The next morning, before Jane set out to Feeney's, she hung out the washing. Fiona heard laughter and, looking out, saw Michael holding up one of Jane's slips with a V-shaped edge of lace along the chest. He took it in his arms, dancing with it. She tried to grab it from him but he put his arms around her, dancing with her now, the wet slip between them.

When Jane came in, she was flushed, her eyes so lit they looked wet. She loaded the pan with rashers and called Michael in, then came up behind Fiona and pressed her cheek to the side of her face.

"Good girl yourself," Jane chattered lightly in Fiona's ear, and kissed her, happy as air.

"You're all wet from the slip." For the fraction of a second, Jane did not breathe. She'd not meet Fiona's eyes, and Fiona felt her struggling to seem inconspicuous, to seem preoccupied with other things, chatting offhandedly when Michael came in, a lilt to her voice, about the new cash register at Feeney's that had a bell and rang every time she punched in a sum.

Jane spoke in a breathless rush. "I'm better at adding

things up in my own head than on a machine. I've always been good at arithmetic. It's a strength of mine. At Presentation I won the blue ribbon for long division."

When Fiona refused the rashers, Jane picked them up off her plate with the tongs and dropped them onto Michael's plate.

"I'll be too full to work, Jane," Michael said. Jane laughed and caught Fiona's eye.

"They got the cash register to make things easier," she said, a note of dismay now discernible in her voice. "But it makes things harder."

Jane shook faintly as she went to the sink and fussed with the dishes. Fiona sensed that she felt guilty for flirting with Michael.

When Michael went out, Jane asked, "Fiona, what's wrong? You're peculiar quiet."

"I told you. I'm trying to concentrate."

Jane paused. Fiona could feel her thinking, struggling to make contact with her.

"You've a lovely face on you, Fiona. You know I used to think you looked like your father, but I see now it's just the coloring that's his. You're so much like me, Fiona."

Fiona met her eyes and found herself unnerved by the way Jane searched her face, the same way she searched her own face in the photograph over the shrine.

"No," Fiona said. "You're wrong. I look like my father."

"You're an Irish beauty," Jane said in a soft, hurt voice, and moved away from her.

Fiona withdrew further from both of them, grateful for the demands of the seed-pearling.

On Jane's insistence, Michael carried the kitchen table and chairs outside for the evening meal.

"Our Michael and his prodigal strength!" Jane cried, and he winked at her.

She set the table, then turned the wireless on loud and faced it out the open kitchen window. The evening air, which presaged summer, was so still she was able to light candles.

The three sat eating, Fiona avoiding Michael's eyes.

"I think it can happen . . . Ned and I. I think sometimes a woman's got to take the bull by the horns."

Jane jumped up from the table and ran inside. "Look what I found today, Fiona!" Wearing a blue-and-silver-sequined shawl, she turned on her heel and posed. "Do you remember this?"

"Yes."

"You were tiny at the time I made this."

"I remember it, though."

"Of course you do. How could you forget a thing so lovely? After we eat, we can dance!" Jane said.

An old air came on, a man's tenor voice lamenting in Irish.

"I'll sit that one out," Jane cried, and she and Michael laughed. She fiddled with her food, took a bite now and again.

"So, Michael. Describe the parlor to me. Where the old cow sits in state."

"It's close in there, like they never open a window! And it smells of decades of cooked mutton!"

"I'd open the windows and let the breezes in!" Jane cried. "What else?"

"Well, the room is full of legacies. Shining things. Silver and crystal." He went on about a painting of Parnell, and a stuffed grouse on the mantel. Fiona watched him. It was a subtle thing she was feeling. It was on the air like a smell. He was the picture of congeniality. Gently at ease in the company of women. And yet, there was something untouchable in him. Elusive. She had not seen it before. She had not suspected such a thing. It occurred to her that there was some secret between Michael and the brown-haired girl, some understanding from which she would always be excluded.

Slowly as she watched him, she put it to words. He didn't love her. Her distress had surfaced within her to a clearly formed thought. Michael didn't love her.

Her rebuffs today had not changed the bravura of his manner. Remembering Beltane, she felt used, and a sensation of hatred concentrated and tightened within her heart.

"So, does Ned dance attendance upon the old cow, Michael?" Jane asked.

"He does."

"Christ!"

There was a pause. Michael's eyes flashed on Fiona, and Jane noticed this. "She's been peculiar quiet with me all day, Michael."

"With me as well," he said.

"What is it, love?" Jane asked, leaning into Fiona.

"I told you already! I'm thinking about the dress. I've loads to do on it!" she cried, unable to hide her irritation.

"I don't believe it's that," Jane said.

Fiona took a deep breath, then cried out suddenly, "It's because you're just getting so wound up about Ned coming at Midsummer! I wish you'd calm a bit in yourself, Mother!"

Jane looked affronted. She stared hard at Fiona, then began

nodding her head. In a quiet voice she said, "Ye just don't want me happy. Ye prefer me miserable!"

"No! I just think you're getting too worked up."

"You're not going to ruin my night! Michael and I are going to have a drink now. If you're going to be a stick-in-the-mud, you can go inside."

"I don't mind," Fiona said, picking up her plate and carrying it in.

She could hear them outside talking and drinking.

Jane said loudly, "Fiona gets moodier the older she gets! She reminds me of the girl with consumption from Presentation! A girl all blood and thunder with the anger, her skin hot and vapory to the touch, like you'd put your finger into the flame of a candle. An hour later she could be so meek you wouldn't think her the same girl. Her skin would be clammy and cold as a piece of dinner china."

Fiona waited to hear what Michael would say, but he remained silent.

"I'll go in and feel her arm in a bit, and if it's as cold as a porcelain, we'll know she'll be civil and I'll invite her back out," Jane said.

Fiona heard a faint laugh from Michael. Soon, though, Jane was back on the subject of Ned McGinty.

"So it was like pulling teeth, was it?"

"It was," Michael said congenially, relieved maybe that they were off the subject of Fiona. "How long had I to go on with him over that blasted indoor pump?"

"It's that way with me and him as well. I don't even bother saying hello to him on Friday nights, but 'How are the hens, laying?'"

The two of them laughed.

A reel played on the wireless. When there was a lull in the music, Fiona could hear them talking again.

"Rome wasn't built in a day!" Michael cried out, and Fiona could hear the alcohol in his voice.

"No, it wasn't," Jane cried. "God knows it wasn't!"

The month of May progressed, Fiona working carefully on her commission, keeping her distance from Michael. She found sustenance in his confusion. Sometimes he sat at the table while she worked. She felt his eyes on her and there was pleasure for her in his fine-tuned attention.

He would have to find a way to bring her back to him. She didn't know how or what he might do. It would not be something he could concoct, but would have to happen spontaneously, she thought.

One day late in May she watched him through the window. As always, he seemed lost in his thoughts while he worked. At first, a certain humility and bafflement present in his expression moved her. But something passed through his mind that made him smile, and he strutted, looking pleased with himself. She felt the muscles in her groin tingle even as she wished she could deprive him of his bravura.

She exhausted herself with her resistance, and when he disappeared into the dairy, she escaped the house and wandered north along the road, stopping at the iron gate before Presentation orphanage, drawn strangely to the gabled monstrosity of female solitudes. She wished she could disappear into its dark halls, remembering the watery echoes within. She wished for Sister Delphine, in the way Jane had once wished for her. She imagined herself in the old nun's arms, listening to the repeated

chanting of her own name in the French accent: "Fiona O'Faolain. Fiona O'Faolain."

Ann Finley, whose mother visited the nuns, said Sister Delphine was very old now. She slept a lot and was wheeled about in
a squeaky iron chair by a younger nun.

Remembering this, Fiona came back to her senses, thinking it was a sad thing that she could long so much for such a miserable place. A sudden wind came up from the sea, infuriating
the alder trees around the orphanage. Fiona thought of the loneliness of women. Of Circe and Calypso. Even as each had reveled
with Odysseus in her bed, she had been aware of the inevitability
of his departure.

She went back and, as she scaled the hill, saw Michael
walking across the yard. He moved toward her and she stopped
in her tracks, dropping her eyes to the ground. As he got closer
to her, she shivered, letting out little halting breaths. In his arms
she felt herself weakening, but when his mouth touched hers,
she saw the brown-haired girl and tore herself loose of him, running inside.

A few mornings later, Jane started the car to go to Feeney's, and
smoke came out from under the hood.

Driving it slowly down the hill, Michael took it to Mr.
Nugent, the mechanic. It was raining when Michael came back,
riding up the hill on an old bicycle covered with rust, the chains
squeaking.

"Look at him, imitating the old man," Jane cried.

"He gave me this so we'd get by a few days without the
car," Michael called out, and they laughed.

He rode it in a circle in front of the house, imitating Mr.
Nugent, who, in spite of being a mechanic for cars, rode a bicy-

cle and always stood upright on the pedals. Michael mimicked
the staccato movement of his legs.

"You clown!" Jane cried.

Michael tipped an imaginary hat to them in the manner of
Mr. Nugent—"Good day to ye!"—then pretended to lose control of the bicycle, steering it jaggedly side to side. "Jayzus! Oh,
Joseph!" he cried. Fiona and Jane split their sides at him, the
three soaked now in the rain.

He rode in close, leaning over and grabbing Fiona, hoisting
her up on the handlebars and driving a jaunty circle, Fiona
squealing to get down, managing her way loose.

"Now's your turn, lassie," he said to Jane, pulling her up
and driving down the rocky hill, the bicycle trembling with the
weight and the rocks.

"Help, Fiona!" Jane cried. "He's gone mad!" By the time
they reached the bottom of the hill, they were flying—straight
across the road into the neglected field across the way, Fiona running after, splashing in the puddles the rain had made in the ragwort and the thistles. The bike toppled sideways, and no sooner
had the two fallen off than Michael was after Fiona again.

"Come here, my girl, and put your haunches up on my
bar!" he cried, still imitating Mr. Nugent.

"He'd never say such a thing!" Fiona cried.

"He'd never say such a thing, but you know he's thinking
it!" Michael said.

"Ye filthy!" Jane cried, breathless and laughing. The two of
them struggled to get the bicycle from Michael, pushing him
until he slipped in the ragwort.

Leading the bicycle, Jane and Fiona ran from the field and
across the road. In the skulduggery, Jane had gotten a cut on her

temple and a little stream of blood ran down, diluting with rivulets of rain on her face.

He overtook them halfway up the hill to the house, wrestling the bike away. They let him have it and ran into the house locking him outside, but he managed to push it hard enough so the screw that held the flimsy lock in place broke loose of the wood.

"Christ Almighty!" Jane cried, wide-eyed with excitement, squeezing Fiona's shoulder.

"God!" Fiona yelled, and they ran into the lavatory, holding the door closed with the weight of their bodies.

He pushed his way in, and when he had them at his mercy, they cowered, laughing in the bathtub.

Jane looked up boldly then and with her hands on her waist said, "And what is it, after all, Mr. Devlin, that you plan to do with us?" Michael hoisted her onto his shoulders and carried her to the bedroom, throwing her onto one of the beds. He came back in for Fiona and did the same with her, then stood in the doorway breathing with exertion, a confused smile on his lips. After an awkward quiet, he turned away and they heard his footsteps as he went out and shut the door. Fiona and Jane looked at each other and burst into laughter.

After they had changed their clothes and sopped the wet up from the floors, Fiona saw Michael outside moving through the field in the rain.

"He's getting himself soaked out there, just wanderin' in the barley like he doesn't even know it's raining," Fiona said, laughing.

Jane went to the door and yelled out to him, "Come in here out of the wet!" She handed him a towel as he came in.

"What were you doing?"

"The plants are even bigger today than yesterday. You have to look at the stalks," he said excitedly as he dried his hair.

"And you couldn't wait for the rain to stop before you looked?"

"Rain doesn't bother me, Jane. You should know that by now."

Jane brought out a bottle of port and a box of Marietta biscuits.

"So, Michael, tell us why you've got such a passion in you for that field," Jane said.

"It was on the festival of Lughnasa, the Harvest, that my mother met my father. They left the dancing together. Children conceived at the Harvest are wed to the land. To the spirit or sovereignty of Ireland herself."

Fiona listened with curiosity and unease to Michael's lore.

"And that's why I put such store in the nurturing of the fields."

He took out his wallet and showed them a black-and-white photograph of his father. It was as if they were looking at Michael himself ten or fifteen years older.

"When my father was a boy, he touched a dolmen stone, which is said to be the stone most deeply buried in the earth. Lua Fail. The stone of destiny. It cried out when he touched it. He was proclaimed to be a kind of king."

"The son of a king, are ye?" Jane asked. "That explains the great handsome beast that you are in yourself, lad."

No one spoke, Fiona and Jane sitting pressed one to the other looking from the photograph to Michael and back again, the room darker and darker with the rain, the noise of it hitting the windows.

Gazing at the photo of his handsome father, Fiona saw Michael when he would be older and found herself wishing that she would be with him still.

"It's Lughnasa is the next festival coming. At summer's end." He picked out an apple from a bowl and bit it, his feet up on the table.

Jane poured them each another glass of port and Michael sang:

> *The snows they melt the soonest when the wind begins to sing,*
> *And the corn it ripens fastest when the frosts are settling in.*

He looked straight at Fiona and his voice infused her.

> *And when a woman tells me that my face she'll soon forget . . .*
> *Before we part I'll wage a crown, she's fain to follow yet.*

Fiona looked down, staring at her hands.

"It's the mature woman is the Harvest Queen." He looked at Jane. "We can put a barley crown on Jane and she can rule the field before it's cut."

Jane laughed, delighted, and a wave of pain moved through Fiona.

Michael leaned toward Jane, dropping the core of his apple down the front of her blouse, and she jumped at the cold of it.

"You rogue!" she cried.

Fiona's heart went fast. She wanted to claim him back from Jane, the two always laughing and joking and close over it. Michael seemed to be reading Fiona's eyes. He finished his glassful, and sang:

And the swallow flies without a thought as long as it is
    spring . . .
But when the spring goes and winter blows, my love then
    you'll be fain,
For all your pride to follow me across the raging main.

He got up and seated himself beside Fiona. His hand closed over hers, and when she allowed it, he let out a breath, a little laugh, which surprised her, so rife was it with relief and happiness.

"Where shall we go?" he whispered into her ear, the feel of his breath sending a chill down her side.

"Out in the barley," she said.

"It's damp out there."

"I don't care." She felt Jane watching and sensed her distress.

Michael stood up and went to the door. "It's stopped raining."

"We're going for a walk," Fiona said. "I'll be back soon."

Jane did not answer, and Fiona and Michael slipped outside into near darkness.

Fiona felt slightly crazed and ran up the wet row of barley, laughing. Soon they were wrestling on the ground. She laughed, trying to slip loose of him, remembering the mare's challenge to the roan stallion. Her thighs resisted him and she got away and ran and he came behind, his hands on her two breasts. Her knees weakened a moment and he said, "Mermaid, you've no legs to support you."

They were on the ground again, and now, like the stallion, he held to her while she fought and soon was in her.

She could feel in the way he was kissing her neck and chest

what the waiting and the uncertainty had done to him. She hadn't anticipated the power of it, but now lying beneath him, she felt intensely receptive to it, knowing he'd risen to her in the right moment, his ache for her transmitted into her body in jolts. She hardly moved, allowing him to ravish her. He seemed not in control of his passions, and she wondered if maybe he did love her. She felt a desire to laugh, a soft jubilation climbing up from the excited, tender places in her toward her throat. She did not hold on to him. She spread her arms straight out on the cold ground. He was the one holding her and she let him. He was still fixing her as if he thought she might escape.

Which sense was it, she wondered, that detected Jane there suddenly watching from the darkness at the end of the row? But only for a moment or two before she was gone again. Had Jane seen, Fiona wondered, how intent Michael was upon her?

When Michael reached his rapture, she wished Jane were there to see how blind and deaf and helpless she made him. She wished Jane could hear him sing out, "Fiona, Fiona!" the softness in his voice. How she stopped him in his power so he could not go on.

Fiona walked Michael down to his cottage and they stood kissing. She pressed a palm to his face. It was late May and they had the entire summer still before them. She felt it now in the dark, an impending shift in the weather, some new wave of life beginning between them.

When Fiona went back inside, Jane was sitting at the table gazing into the ruby liquid in her glass. And though it looked as if she'd been crying, a small smile was on her mouth. Fiona sat with her. They were quiet awhile before Jane looked up at her.

"Jayzus, love. He's a great beauty."

"Yes," Fiona said, and smiled at her.

"He could fill a girl with a great weakness, could he not?" Jane's lips were dark with the wine, and the color was up in her cheeks.

"He could, Mother."

TWELVE

A bluster came up inland from the ocean the day before Midsummer and Ned's appointed tea. Jane opened all the windows and the door, the wind carrying on its back the smells of the meadowsweet flourishing wild on the roadsides.

Twice Jane washed a tablecloth with raised chenille roses and new linen napkins to get the stiffness out of them. She churned a new pot of butter and formed it into a rosette on the top.

Everything outside was rampant and in flower. Insects, unable to navigate the breeze, were carried off on its currents. A strong gust blew one of the errant hens into the kitchen, and Jane had to chase it out with the broom.

She began preparations on a steak and kidney pie, a lemon jelly, and a salad of potatoes, beetroot, and dandelion flowers. If Ned was confused by the flowers, she told Fiona, she'd explain to him that Sister Delphine had told her they were a delicacy in France.

In the late afternoon she varnished the floor so thoroughly that their shoes stuck to it when it dried. She made Fiona tiptoe barefoot anytime she had to cross the room.

All day she mortified herself by not eating a bite of food, and near evening Fiona saw her standing under the alder trees down near the road, a fisted hand to her forehead.

Every few hours that night, Fiona awakened, overwhelmed by the smells of soap and varnish, which had become infused for her with Jane's anxiety. Jane's bed remained empty all night, and Fiona saw her kneeling before her shrine pleading with the Virgin Mother, the candles stirring and guttering frantically in a breeze through one open window.

But the next morning she sat coolly at the table smoking a cigarette and seemed in full possession of herself as she penciled out the day's tasks ahead of her, mapping them into a kind of order.

As the hour neared, presence of mind abandoned her. It occurred to Jane that he might not come. Unable to wait and see, she dispatched Michael to fetch him. Fiona watched out the window and saw them coming.

"He's dressed in his Sunday clothes," Fiona announced with relief, an indication that he had intended to come.

Escorted by Michael, Ned moved clumsily into the room, lowering his head and narrowing his shoulders, as if he were remembering the day long ago when he'd been crowded into the car with them. He did not offer a nod or utter a hello, his expression grave. Jane took his jacket and Michael pulled out the chair, gesturing for him to sit. With an easy, engaging manner, Michael brought him around, going straight into farming talk.

"What type of hens are those that you have?"

"Rhode Island Reds. We're partial to them."

"Why?"

"They're smaller so they eat less. But they lay a good-sized egg."

"And how are they producing?"

"Good." Ned nodded. "Good."

"Take a bit of port with your tea, Ned," Michael said, filling his own glass as if in encouragement.

Ned nodded assent.

He kept averting his eyes from Jane's and Fiona's. He was relieved to receive a plate of food and began to eat.

"I know how much you like steak and kidney pie," Jane said, standing behind his chair, her chest puffing up.

When he turned to her with a questioning look, she said, "You told me once, you goose! You behave as if I know nothing about you, Ned McGinty. You forget I've known you for ages."

She flitted busily around him. When she added hot tea to his cup after he'd taken only one sip, he winced faintly and Fiona felt a pulse of empathy for him.

Throughout the meal Michael took charge of keeping the conversation afloat, and when he'd run dry of things to talk about, he resorted to mentioning the dreaded indoor pump. Ned's eyes lit up, and closing out Jane and Fiona, he went on about the pump, whose working confounded and preoccupied him. "I've never seen a bolt like it. I haven't been able to find a matching part. I tried soldering one."

"I may have something you can use instead," Michael said.

Fiona could see Jane growing dismayed. Ned went into a litany on the various sizes and shapes of bolts and screws.

"Now," Jane said, interrupting him suddenly. "Enough talk about hardware for the love of God!"

Ned blinked and silenced. Quiet held the air. Nervously Jane mentioned the cash register at Feeney's.

Fiona saw Ned's eyes change suddenly. He was looking beyond Jane's shoulder at the framed photograph of her at sixteen, hanging near the shrine. Jane saw him looking at it, too, her eyes large as saucers.

"Do you remember me as I was then, Ned?" Jane asked, pointing to the picture.

A moment of breathless silence held the two of them before Ned dropped his eyes to the tablecloth. He colored as if he had been slapped.

Fiona squeezed Michael's hand under the table. They exchanged a look and Michael rose.

"I'm stuffed," he said.

Fiona stood also, following suit.

Ned looked at the three of them, understanding the plan of action, as if it were a conspiracy against him.

"I've got to be off," Ned said angrily, pushing his chair from the table.

"Oh, no!" Michael cried. "You stay on a bit longer, Ned. Have another glass of port."

"No, no. I'm off. Can you lend me that yoke you told me about? You know, for the pump."

"Will you come back then?" Jane asked.

"Not likely today," Ned said, not looking at her, and he was out the door, Michael on his heels.

"Oh, Jayzus," Jane whispered. "I thought it would be good for him to see that picture, that it would remind him of when he loved me."

"He doesn't forgive you," Fiona said. "You must have wounded him to the quick."

"Oh, God! He must have loved me so much! I can hardly bear to think about what I did to that man!"

"You ought to admit you hurt him and say you're sorry! Bring it out in the open," Fiona barked. "It's still festering in him."

Jane looked at her, chastised.

"You're as bad as he is. Why don't you be straight with him? Why all the silly simpering. He doesn't like it, you know. I was watching him."

Later, before dark, Jane went down to the fence between their properties when she saw Ned driving the sheep into their pen. He strolled over when she beckoned to him. Fiona could not hear what she was saying to him, but she was weeping and going on for a while, in a confessional manner, everything seeming to pour forth from her in a river. She held on to his hands and he listened with a lowered head.

Fiona and Michael were sitting at the table when Jane came back in, sniffling, but easier.

"He listened to me." Jane sat down, wiping tears from her face. "He'll work on the old woman, he says. He'll get her to have me over for tea, so she and I can just talk."

"She'll be the harder nut to crack," Fiona said.

*

In the middle of the night, Fiona awakened, sensing someone else in the house. With a frightened heart she moved into the front room where a lamp was lit. Before he sensed her there, Fiona saw Michael barely breathing, leaning toward the photograph of Jane.

"God on earth!" he cried when he saw her come into the light.

"What are you doing?"

"Come down with me." He touched Fiona's hair. "Come down and sleep with me."

In the month of July, the barley grew high and lush, the field prolific.

Some nights Fiona slept in Michael's cottage, and from his window she could hear Jane's wireless faintly from above. If she peered out, she could see Jane sitting on a chair near the open kitchen door, smoking a cigarette. Jane spent her days moving mindlessly through her chores, far away, waiting. She collected eggs and often forgot to take them out of her apron pockets until one would break, the yolk leaking through.

Ned reassured her on Friday nights at the Moon and the Stars, saying that the old woman had agreed to meet with her and he was pressing her to choose a day.

In mid-July they started pulling up the cabbages. Fiona could hardly get a knife through one, they were so dense and heavy, a great labor to chop. But each one yielded a veritable mountain of shreds. The days were drowsy and sunny, the chickens skulking and the cows lying in the grass wheezing softly.

After Martha Hanrahan and the three bridesmaids came for a final fitting, Fiona put the last touches on the four dresses, and

Jane said that she was glad that the crowd of them would soon be leaving. That they were a noisy lot with all that tulle brushing jealously at the satin. With the dresses full-blown, it was as bad as having the four bitches themselves in the kitchen.

Michael helped Fiona move the dresses on their forms outside and stand them in front of the fuchsia hedge at the roadside where she photographed them in good light.

That same afternoon Martha and the three others came, a parade of cars, each dress carefully wrapped and prepared for transport, carried and laid like invalids across backseats. And the wedding gown laid out in the trunk of Mr. Hanrahan's Ford as if in a dead faint.

It was a Wednesday afternoon when Ned waved Jane down, calling her to the fence between their properties, where they spoke a few moments and he squeezed her hand.

Jane came back to the house, agitated. Mrs. McGinty had decided on the coming Sunday. One o'clock. Jane would go there on her own.

Perhaps it was seeing the dresses out in the sunlight that inspired her to ask Michael to help her unearth the Giantess from the depths of the closet. Or perhaps it was the possibility of herself being a bride looming more real. He helped her push the magnificent dress, still on its form, between the two small beds and out into the middle of the kitchen.

A silence held the air. In the overcast daylight, and in an area wide enough so that it could spread its skirts to full sweep, the gown appeared a vulnerable mythic thing; a chimera. It had never been fully visible before, pressed into the dim of the closet and only seen in sections. The full effect stunned Fiona, catching light in thousands of clear and silver beads.

It breathed a white, arboreal coolness into the room, and an aroma faintly sacramental, like candle wax and exotic wood. It seemed to quiver in its new exposure, as if composed of living tissue, an elaborate multifaceted flower, a monument to Jane's desire. Fiona wanted to cry at the strange purity of the thing.

"When I was at Presentation," Jane said in a meek voice, "I once stitched a dead mouse into the layers of one of Sister Elma's wedding dresses and no one suspected. Ye could put a dead calf into this one and who would know?" She seemed genuinely mystified by her own creation, her face damp and pink and almost embarrassed as she looked at it.

They sat awhile in silence as if before an enigma.

"It's a castle in the air," Jane whispered.

Once the shock of its presence had settled slightly, Fiona knelt before it and gingerly examined its architecture. What had originally been the simpler mantua, petticoat, and court train of Catherine Heavey's dress, Jane had renovated by breaking and resetting seams, adding layers and panels all swollen with embroidery, floral and foliate motifs in polychrome silver thread, encrusted in places with crystals, and edged in ruffles dense as carnations.

She had gored and regored the main skirt, adding more fabric to accommodate the wide bell cage she'd put beneath to increase the width. The reset seams she had hidden beneath thick silk piping and platinum braid.

"It seems almost strange to remember what things once were and what they eventually become," Fiona said, recalling the slimmer sheath of Catherine Heavey's dress.

"It's desire fuels such a creation," Michael said, looking at the dress. "It's passion."

Jane stopped breathing. After a moment she said, "And the

field, too. Remember the field before it was plowed? And look at it now. We could get lost in it for days."

"Lughnasa's coming," Michael said. "You can smell the change on the air. The field is almost ready to be cut." He looked dreamily at the sky through the window. "Summer's end."

A wave of sadness moved through Fiona. Michael seemed far away from her.

"God, I'm frightened about Sunday. About meeting with the old woman," Jane said.

"Why don't we take a drive to the shore?" Michael asked. "We'll go south. Maybe to Cashel Bay."

The sky remained bright as they drove. But the mood went with them. Michael seemed full of some lofty anticipation about the world, a contagion to his spirit.

He parked near the sea and they spent the afternoon walking the long strand to its end where cliffs jutted out and the water exploded against the rock.

When the sun disappeared, they pressed back against a blustering wind, heads and bodies bowed, their arms linked. At the end of the strand they climbed a ways up to the road and went into the isolated Elen Hotel, which overlooked the sea, and into its restaurant for an early dinner. Jane oohed and ahhed over the atmosphere of the room, touching the red tablecloths and the gold filigree on the menus.

The woman from the desk, who wore thick glasses and had an odd, overquick manner, came in to them as they were having coffee and pointed down to the strand. "I'm Mrs. O'Toole," she said in a nasally voice. "I'm on management duty today. Are ye having a pleasant time?"

"Yes, very much," Jane said, enjoying the role of patron.

"Do you see that there in the tides?" Mrs. O'Toole asked, pointing out the window.

"It looks like a sheep," Fiona said.

"It is. And if you squint your eyes and look way past, you'll see another one there, washing back and forth."

"We were just walking down there and didn't see a thing."

"You must have just missed them. It's this hour of the day when they usually come in with the tide."

"Why?" Michael asked, standing a moment to get a better look.

"There's a farmer who grazes his herd up there on a cliff," Mrs. O'Toole said, her eyes like cloudy pools, enlarged behind the thick of her glasses. "And something compels the sheep to throw themselves into the sea. It's unnerving, an odd thing about this place. Some say it's evil faeries take possession of them and drive them mad. Others say that particular farmer's sheep have no depth perception. That it's a problem with the breeding."

Fiona felt as if she were going to burst into laughter, but the woman took herself so seriously that she didn't dare.

"It's devilish shocking when the sodden creatures come rushing in with the foam, and the tide leaving them so at the feet of the tourists. I've seen Americans take photographs of the godforsaken creatures. Can ye imagine? Having their children pose with a drowned sheep, its eyes rolled back in its head, for the love of God?" She drew in air and made the sign of the cross.

Fiona noticed that Jane was working to suppress a smile and kept her eyes averted from the woman's.

But Michael, enticed by the sport the old woman presented, kept engaging Mrs. O'Toole with questions.

"And which theory is it you believe, missus?"

"I'm more of the evil faery theory."

"Are ye now? Have ye seen the evil manifesting itself in other ways around here?"

"Oh, yes! I'm not from here, of course. I'm from Carleford. In Carleford you'd never see such things as you see here. The madness that gets into people when they live so close to the sea." She paused. "You don't yourselves come from a place so near the sea, do ye?"

"Oh, no, missus. And we find that, too, my sisters and myself," Michael said, pointing to Jane and Fiona. "Something odd in people's eyes when they live too near the sea."

Fiona couldn't bear it any longer and excused herself and went into the pub to find a table. The others followed in shortly after, Mrs. O'Toole having returned to her desk at the arrival of two more guests.

"It's devilish shocking," Michael said with Mrs. O'Toole's intonations, "when the sodden creatures wash up in the tide!"

Jane laughed hard, leaning her head into Michael's chest.

He ordered glasses of lager and they drank, getting tipsy, Michael relentless on the subject of the suicidal sheep. Once when they'd all quieted their laughing, Michael leaned into Jane, putting his arm around her, and said, "There now, missus. There now." Jane's eyes were closed, a small, rapt smile on her face, flushed and damp with laughing.

The pub door opened onto the small hotel lobby. Fiona noticed Mrs. O'Toole's reflection in a mirror on the wall, watching them archly. She had to lean at an extreme angle from behind the front desk to see them reflected in the mirror. Fiona pointed her out to the others.

When Mrs. O'Toole understood that she'd been spotted, she withdrew her head suddenly so she couldn't be seen.

"Let's drive her mad," Michael said, putting his arm around both Jane and Fiona, giving them both kisses.

"Stop it!" Fiona said, but Jane was smiling, happy to play along.

Appalled, the little woman entered the pub and gave them a fierce-eyed stare. "Heathens!" she cried.

"Can't sisters draw a bit of comfort from their brother?" Jane asked boldly, fearlessly.

Fiona joined in, putting her arm around Michael.

"Scandalous!" the woman cried. "If my uncle were here tonight, I'd have the lot of you thrown out for indecency!"

"We're just having it on with you, Missus O'Toole," Michael said. "Come and join us. What might we buy you to drink?"

The fierceness in her eyes dissolved all at once. "A gin and lime."

Michael drew another chair up to the table and ushered her into it.

She regaled them that night with the loss of her husband at an early age. "He defected to France!" she cried after her second drink.

"Defected from what?" Michael asked her.

"I don't know," she said, lifting her glass. "He just defected!"

"Did you drive him to it, Missus O'Toole, demanding jewels and furs?"

"Bounder!" she cried, laughing. "This one's a bounder," she said to Jane. "Oh, you two have your hands full with this one."

After her third, Mrs. O'Toole told them about a ghost that lived in a hotel to the south, the ghost of a German. Now and then he appeared to distressed travelers in a particular room. The ghost had a question it wanted answered, but no one it appeared to understood German, "and the poor creature has no peace. Three centuries it's been speaking German to the Irish, and none can sort out what it's trying to ask."

Again, Mrs. O'Toole's tone, all earnest seriousness, had the three of them in tears and herself not minding the effect she had, the gin making her own eyes watery. She excused herself now and then to greet a guest or to answer the telephone in the lobby.

They decided to take two rooms in the hotel, all of them too full of the drink to drive, and it slashing rain now outside, making the coastal roads slippery.

Once when Jane left the table to go to the lavatory, Fiona took Michael's hand.

"Should I come to you in the night?" she asked softly.

"Yes."

Upstairs, Fiona and Jane lay side by side in a double bed. In spite of the pattering rain they had opened the window so they could listen to the sea below.

"Don't worry, Mother," Fiona said, sensing Jane's anxiety about the approaching day.

"I know you want to go in to Michael, Fiona, but will you stay until I fall asleep?"

"Yes."

"I'll appeal to the woman in Mrs. McGinty. Somewhere in that hardened old creature the memory of a romantic nature must still exist."

"Yes," Fiona whispered.

*

While waiting, Fiona fell into a slumber and dreamed that Jane
had slipped from bed and was herself going in to Michael. Fiona
started and woke, finding Jane beside her.

She lay listening for a long time, waiting for Jane's breath
to change in sleep, remembering the dress. It was too large
somehow for this world and, in spite of its opulence, seemed
somehow helpless. Jane's passions, Fiona thought, were slippery
and without boundaries. Multifaceted.

When she thought Jane was asleep, she rose to go to
Michael, and as she was nearing the door, Jane said through the
darkness, "Go to him, love."

Fiona paused at the door uncertainly. "Mother," Fiona said,
moving back toward the bed in the dark. "I'll wait."

"It's all right. Go to him."

Fiona stood without breathing, only faintly able to make
out her mother's face.

"Dear God, love," Jane whispered, and Fiona felt her hand
on her forearm, "go to him."

"I'm only going to the lavatory. I'll be right back." Fiona
went to the toilet and then returned.

"You see," she said, getting back into bed. She listened a
long time in the dark, but Jane's breathing did not change. She
kept thinking uneasily of the dream. Her heart sped up. She got
quietly out of bed. As she was closing the door, she heard Jane
say her name softly, but she pretended not to hear.

Fiona lay back on Michael's bed and he bent over her. She could
feel faint twinges in one of her ovaries and knew she was fertile
tonight, and she wished that Michael was not so attuned to that,
not so nervous and careful of it. He would manage the lovemak-

ing, prevent any chance of pregnancy. But she wished for it now, a part of him inhabiting her.

"Soon'll be time to bring down the harvest," he whispered fervently as if it were part of the excitement between them. "The barley field's a beautiful thing, and the potato flowers." His eyes were half-closed, his voice velvety with delirium.

She was only the touchstone of something larger; his excitement spread to the damp earth yielding its fruits up to him; the reaping of what he'd sown. She felt herself only on the periphery of his heart.

"There will be more fires. We'll dance," he said, kneeling over her, kissing her breasts, her stomach.

"The grain is swollen now, the shoots are unfurling." He kissed the mound of her sex and she let herself surrender to the pleasure of his tongue. It was still raining outside and the wetness of the air was sweet to her. Her own sighs sounded dry and soft like the noise of wind brushing barley.

The sadness deepened the more aroused she became until the moment she seemed to rise out of herself, complicit with the curtain that billowed on the air above him.

THIRTEEN

The harvest was beginning, their own fields ready before any of the neighboring ones. At dusk, unfamiliar men moved through the barley carrying lamps.

Fiona put out piles of scones and sliced loaf cake on a trestle table set up in front of the house. She boiled kettles for the men, two tinkers, named Big John and Martin, and Michael's cousin Eamon. Big John was a lumbering man who sucked down a cup of tea in two swallows, who ate a scone with one hand while pocketing one with the other.

There was tons of cake, Jane experimenting with the sultana loaf she planned to bring to Mrs. McGinty, trying it with two eggs, and then with three. With vanilla or with essence of rum. Some of the loaves failed, but Big John visited the trestle table regularly and ate them anyhow, collapsed or burned or doughy at the center.

He did not go to the outhouse like the other men, and once Fiona came upon him pissing freely against the stones at the side of the house. Unperturbed, he nodded his head in greeting to her as if they were passing each other on the road. She'd started at the sight, the buttons of his shirt straining and from between them thick tufts of chest hair sprouting.

"It's an enchanted field," Fiona heard him say to Michael once. "It's like the loaves and the fishes. So much, so closely packed."

Of all the cups Fiona set out for them in front of the house, Big John always went for the eggshell porcelain, the daintiest, yellow with tiny sprays of violets along the edge. He drank from it with his thick, soiled fingers holding it delicately, saucer on one palm.

The first time Fiona heard the scythes she felt something rend itself softly loose in her chest. The stalks sighed as they fell and the air smelled of green shadows. Martin, the tinker man in charge of huddling the stalks, arranged them into stooks, gathered and tied, standing them upright in the cut field, the heads of the grain pointing skyward.

Sunday morning as Jane prepared to go to Mrs. McGinty, a neighboring boy appeared at the door with a message.

Fiona read it aloud to Jane. "Am under the weather today. Will select a new date. Thank you, Attracta McGinty."

Jane stopped the comb in her hair.

"No matter," she whispered with resolution, and continued to comb. "I'm going anyhow. I was almost expecting that message from the old woman, Fiona."

"You're still going?"

"I am. How many years has it been that that old bitch won't let me into her parlor? I'm bringing her the cake. Come with me, love."

Jane had wrapped it in red glassine paper and tied it with pink satin ribbon. She carried it ceremoniously before her, hands cupped beneath it.

The top half of the McGinty door was slightly ajar. Jane pushed it open and they could see directly into the parlor. Mrs. McGinty, a rosary wrapped around her wrist, was asleep in an overstuffed chair supported by bunting and an arrangement of pillows. The room was clean and well dusted but crowded with bric-a-brac.

Jane knocked and the old woman stirred. She coughed and squirmed to sit, her eyes widening on Jane.

"Did you not get my message, Miss O'Faolain?" The old woman's voice was deep and wizened sounding.

"I did, Mrs. McGinty, but I've labored over this cake," Jane said, leaning in through the open top half of the door, showing her the brightly wrapped package. "I've made certain it was something you could find no fault with and I want you to have it."

"Not today, Miss O'Faolain."

Jane paused and in a soft voice said, "I can assure you it's very moist, missus."

The old woman's focus deepened. She struggled to sit up higher in her pillowed chair.

"It's a sultana cake," Jane said.

"I don't eat sultanas."

"Your son says that you do."

"You've got a lot of cheek, talking to me so."

"I only want you to accept my gift."

"I don't forget the shameless way you treated my son years back."

"I've apologized for that. I regret that."

The old woman held Jane's eyes. "I know your real motives. You want my son to pick you up out of the bog you were born in."

Fiona froze.

The old woman's eyes glossed, mineral dark. "You want him to give you status. Your own mother in the pauper's grave. Do you think he wants responsibility of an illegitimate daughter, likely following in her own mother's footsteps?"

Fiona felt the hurt ribboning from Jane in waves.

"My son may dance with you on a Friday night, but he won't marry you. You have notions that he will but you're dead wrong. He'll never go against me."

The old woman pursed her mouth, watching Jane like a hawk.

"How dare you speak—" Fiona began to cry out, but Jane squeezed her forearm to silence her. Jane stared into the air before her as if something was becoming clear. At last when she spoke she said calmly, "You judge my own mother, a slip of a girl, because she was buried in a pauper's grave."

"Go away," the old woman said.

"And you . . . smotherin' the life out of your own son."

The old woman made an angry, dismissive gesture.

Jane fumbled, looking for a place to put the cake down. She set it on the step, then turned, raising her hands before her, feeling the air a moment as if she could not see. She walked up the path and through the gate, Fiona following.

At home, Jane did not cry, but sat and stared and smoked.

Fiona told Michael what had happened, and that night at the meal he watched Jane's face as she moved her food around with her fork and whispered to herself as if she were alone in the room.

She looked up once and pointed at the Giantess, still crowding the far corner of the room. "I don't want that anymore."

Fiona and Michael exchanged a look.

"What'll we do with it, Jane?" Michael asked her softly, leaning toward her.

She looked into his face, as if moved by the sound of his voice. "I don't know, Michael, but I don't want it anymore."

That night Fiona slept fitfully. She woke once and saw that Jane was not in bed. She found her in the kitchen sitting very still in her chair. She seemed to be concentrating, given over to some interior image, panting faintly as if her thoughts excited her.

"Mother, are you all right?"

Jane did not answer so Fiona sat down across from her, squinting in the lamplight, struggling to read the expression on her mother's face, which seemed to presage both laughter and tears.

"Are you all right?"

Jane nodded and looked faintly irritated, as if she were being interrupted, torn away from another place.

Fiona felt dizzy. She noticed something unsettling about the air in the room, a faintly rotten odor to the light itself as if the oil in the lamp had gone bad. She lifted the glass flue and sniffed at it and the fumes made her eyes hurt. She closed it and looked again at her mother.

Jane seemed once again oblivious of Fiona. Her eyes glowed as if she were undergoing some transformation, besieged by the power of it; held unmoving in its thrall.

She whispered something Fiona could not decipher, shook her head faintly, and looked down into her hands.

On Monday it poured and the men gathered under the tarp near the road. Michael came down. It looked as if it would be soft weather all day, so he sent them away. He told Fiona he had to deliver fifty bushels the following day to a buyer ready to pay in Galway, and that he would leave Eamon in charge. But today he was going to rest, exhausted by the unremitting labor.

She went to him in the afternoon while he slept. He turned toward her and she kissed his neck and shoulders, embracing him, and he opened his eyes, seeming as if he might rouse to her, but then let go. He explained to her that he was tired, but she said, "It's something more, isn't it."

"Not at all."

"I feel it."

He paused and said that the harvest strained on him and cost him and affected his mood. That in the waning year heat and light lose strength and withdraw. "It changes a man's constitution," he said. They'd have Lughnasa dancing in another few days and his spirits would revive. Just before the field was full cut.

The world felt strange to her, uncertain. She wanted the comfort of him and agonized with desire, would not relent. She touched him in ways that weakened him and brought him around.

She wanted his seed inside her. She wanted him to fill her womb with liquid silk. But though they reveled together, he'd not come inside her, as if he could smell the fertility on her skin.

That evening the weather cleared and Michael called the men to work. Jane wandered out of the kitchen, gazing down the hill at Eamon and Martin lighting lamps, preparing to resume the scything. Fiona stepped out after.

"Have ye Gypsy blood in ye, missus?" a deep voice asked, startling them both.

Big John was standing against the wall of the house with his arms crossed, looking at Jane, a cigarette between his lips. Jane peered at him, faintly startled.

"My own father may have been a Gypsy for all I know of him," she answered.

"He surely was and that's a thing to be proud of." Jane held his eyes, her own lit up by the regard in the man's voice.

"John," Michael called out from the barley, and the big man threw aside his cigarette and went down the hill to the field.

Fiona slept poorly again that night, the sighs of the barley as it fell, and the voices of the men in the field, threading through her dreams. In the deep of night she got up and found Jane again in the kitchen, this time asleep, lying on her arms at the table. The box with Jane's "memories," as she called them, the box she had always kept stored under her bed, sat open, as if she'd been rifling through it for something, leaving things in disarray.

Fiona peered into the box, looking at its contents. Under a chapel veil of wobbly, poorly done lace, she found a small loom made of fish bones, delicate and stained, and the framed photograph of Sister Delphine. She unfolded what she thought would be a handkerchief or a scarf and found it to be a tiny shirt for a girl of four or five years, the crest of Presentation School on one pocket, the fabric deeply worn, grayed with age and wear. A wave of reluctant pity moved through her as she looked at the garment. She folded it again and lay it where she'd found it.

She spotted a red candle half-burned and a wine bottle: keepsakes from Ronan. A pair of blue glass earrings. A lock of Ronan's hair. The nightgown Jane had worn when Ronan would come to her years back, the one of thin gauze, flecks of color all over it. Fiona remembered Jane trying to cast a spell with it, washing it back and forth in the river at Athlone. In a large envelope between papers for the house and Fiona's birth certificate, she found other photographs Ronan had taken of Jane on the beach that fateful day.

Fiona had always thought it was just the three photos, the one that hung near the Virgin's shrine and the two others she'd seen of Jane running in the tide. There were three more. In one Jane stood in profile, naked, arms stretched out behind her holding her dress in both hands so it ballooned in the wind like the sail of a ship, her torso arching forward so you could count the shadows of her ribs under her visible breast.

The second was a closer shot of her from the waist up facing the camera, and the drops of water on her skin so clear, like fine glass beads, each casting a shadow.

In the third, Jane lay naked on the wet sand, the tide retreating, propped up on her elbows facing the camera with a soft, receptive expression, the shadow of her maiden hair visible.

Even after Fiona had put everything back as it had been, she could not forget those three images of Jane. The pictures that

preceded the moments of her own conception. Jane's soft face
before Fiona. The girl she had once been. The loss Jane had not
recovered from.

Early the next morning, Fiona heard the truck's engine as
Michael left with the first of the barley for Galway.

When she got up and went into the kitchen, the sunlight
flooded the corner where the Giantess stood. The window had
been left ajar and a breeze came through, causing the less encum-
bered layers of fabric to shiver.

When Jane walked in, she squinted, recoiling from the
brightness of the dress. She looked away before casting another
uneasy look at it. A fresh gust swept in and the sleeves seemed to
struggle under the weight of their ornamentation as if gesturing
to Jane.

Big John and Martin were soon outside the house waiting
on their food.

Fiona hurried with the kettle. Jane was taking down cups
and saucers when they heard the soft pounding of a bodhran.

"Christ! He brought his drum," Fiona said.

Jane's eyes widened and she stepped out into the doorway,
eyeing the big man.

"A bit of dancing will keep the blood circulating in the
cold," he said to her. Jane snapped her fingers and moved her
head giddily to the beats of his bodhran. "Ye've a Gypsy woman's
spirit."

Jane squeezed her mouth tight to suppress a smile. She
winked at Big John and tossed her head flirtatiously. He bowed
to her, pressed a hand to his heart, and pretended to swoon.

"If I asked you, John, you'd dance a hornpipe for me,
wouldn't you?"

"I'd do that and more if you asked me."

Martin looked on with a kind of sly amusement, and Fiona imagined they'd probably talked of Jane the night before while they'd drank around the fire, and that Big John had intentions.

"Can I ask you a favor, John?" Jane asked.

"Milady," the big man said, curtsying.

She laughed, taking his arm and bringing him into the house. "If you carry this outside for me, you can have it." She pointed to the Giantess. "Maybe you can sell it."

"Mother!" Fiona cried. Jane stiffened at the sound of her voice.

"Are ye serious, missus?" Big John asked. "Such a beautiful thing!"

"I don't want it," Jane said lightly. "It's crowding my little house."

"Ah, you're toyin' with me, missus!"

"I'm not. I'm dead serious."

Big John called Martin in and the two men examined it excitedly.

"Don't you think you might fetch yourselves a pretty penny for this?" Jane asked, her hands on her hips.

"I'd hardly know where to sell such a thing," Big John said half under his breath.

"You can't just give it to them!" Fiona cried. Again Jane did not acknowledge her and Fiona sensed that Jane wished she wasn't there, as if Fiona's presence hindered her somehow.

"Think of it as a gift, John. Sell it and make yourself a little bundle of money."

"I'm a bit afraid to touch it," Big John said with wide eyes.

"Don't be. Put your arms around it like it was a woman and carry her off. You're up to that, I'm sure of it."

Big John gave Jane a roguish smile and hoisted the thing up into his arms, maneuvering it out the door and standing it upright on its form in the light of day.

"Ah, sure, she's in good hands," Jane said.

Fiona followed at a distance as the two men carried it down the hill, crossing the road.

Eamon, who was sitting before a fire, got up from a rock and let out a wild laugh at the men struggling with the dress and settling it finally next to the caravan.

"What are two rough and ready men like yourselves doing with a yoke like this?" He let out another incredulous laugh. In spite of her confusion and her wildly beating heart, Fiona suddenly saw the oddness of the situation and found Eamon's laughter contagious.

"We might sell such a thing at the Puck Fair," John said.

"People shop for horses at the Puck Fair," Eamon cried. "No one there'd be in the market for a dress fit for a bleedin' faery queen." Eamon winked at Fiona, and she smiled.

"Where will we store it so we don't destroy the fine workmanship?" Martin asked.

"We'll have to shift things around so it will fit in the caravan," Big John said.

"God! Think of the terror of waking with such a thing standin' near your bed. I'll not get used to it," Martin said.

Big John constructed a kind of makeshift tent around the dress, using sticks and a tarp.

"Ye might unload that in Dublin, at one of the theaters," Eamon said.

"The Gaiety Theatre near Stephen's Green," Big John cried. "Jayzus God! If they won't have it, what'll we do with the likes of it?"

Eamon and Fiona looked at each other and burst into fresh laughter.

Enlivened by it all, Eamon strutted and said, "Your man's not here today. I vote we discuss this at the pub over a few jars."

"Why not?" Big John asked them, stepping back from the dress, but still eyeing it with a terrible seriousness. "No one to stop us."

Eamon threw a few handfuls of dirt at his fire and it went low. As the three men walked off toward town, Eamon turned and winked again at Fiona. When they were further up the road, Fiona heard Martin say, "We could build a wagon for it. Put it on display and charge people two shillings to see it!"

Fiona gazed after them, dismayed that they were going.

Alone with the dress, she felt the humor leave her. A breeze came up and separated the tarp like a curtain, so she glimpsed the dress where it stood at a slight angle, the form having been placed on crooked earth. It appeared bewildered, this creature so long doted over, protected and kept hidden from the eyes of the world, the creature synonymous with Jane's heart, startled to find itself turned out into the elements.

In some sense Fiona was relieved that the dress would be gone and began to reconcile herself to the idea. As she turned to walk back across the road, a gust came up and she heard a crackling sound. Looking back, she saw the wind knocking the tarp off the dress and the sticks collapsing. The dress teetered as if it might fall, but righted itself, aided by the intricate structure of the skirts. A second, stronger gust revived Eamon's fire and the flames, bending sideways in its current toward the dress, caught at the hems.

Fiona walked quickly back toward it, thinking she might

somehow put out the fire, but she found herself mesmerized by the way the thing took the flame and then burned, slowly and like a lantern, oily drifts of smoke rising from it like veils, ascending and disappearing. A layer of sequins popped as it blackened. It was only that underlayer, Fiona knew, with the crisp fabric, dry as twigs, keeping the thing burning at all, the years of ornamentation and embroidery slow to kindle. Human skin imparted oils to the surface of fine fabric, and the dress was unctuous with Jane's labors, her ministrations.

Fiona looked up toward the house and saw Jane walking slowly down toward her. She stopped a few yards from Fiona, staring gravely at the dress. Gritting her teeth, Fiona resisted an urge to yell at her, to blame her for the dress's demise.

"They should have put it inside," Jane said, kneading a dishcloth absently in her hands. "They were careless."

"What did you expect a couple of tinker men to do with it?" Fiona cried.

The sky darkened and the wind blew suddenly hard, the flames growing roisterous, lapping and twisting. A template of hard glass beads and crystals along the bodice resisted the fire, glowing brightly from within. Grief flooded Fiona at the terrible beauty of the thing, the loss of it. But the emotion on Jane's face seemed to dissipate the longer she stood there. She was not even focused on the dress anymore, Fiona noticed, her eyes on the horizon past it.

When at last Jane turned and ascended the hill back up to the house, smoke rising from the dress drifted after her.

Fiona stayed for a long time biding with the dress, watching it transform. Afterward, with the wind gone, it still stood, a perfect carbon replica of what it had once been. The shadow of the white chimera. The ash of the lily. Fiona gazed at it with the same wonder with which she had studied its moist, white predecessor.

She stepped close to it and, with a single finger, touched it at the chest and the entire thing collapsed, the bits of metal from the dressform clanking down against the stones, the ash falling in a dense heap while some of it swirled wildly in the air.

When the men returned from the pub, Fiona explained to them what had happened. Big John had a philosophical look on his face, enhanced, Fiona was sure, by the alcohol he'd just consumed. Eamon screamed with laughter, and Martin fumed, chasing him and yelling about the carelessness of leaving a fire burning.

As Fiona scaled the hill, the wireless was playing "Have You Seen My Little Seamus?"

Jane's box of memories was open again at the table and she stood before the mirror wearing the gauze nightgown. It still fit, though it strained now at the hips and across the belly. The lace at the hem was torn.

Thunder sounded and Jane ran outside, wrestling her clean slips and dainties from the clothesline. The rain fell suddenly and Fiona looked out the window. In the daylight, overcast though it was, the thin nightgown Jane wore was rendered transparent. Fiona could see her nipples through it, the triangular thatch of her pubic hair. She saw the men before Jane did. One of them must have spotted her first and then called the others over. She seemed to sense their eyes on her and turned. Eamon, Big John, and Martin on the periphery of the field, still as horses, staring at her.

Jane faced them, staring back, her nightgown growing more insignificant in the increasing rain, clinging to her like another layer of skin, the wet ropes of her hair pressing hard to her shoulders, rain splashing mud over her naked ankles and feet. Thunder sounded softly from above. Jane raised her head to the sky and Fiona saw her laugh and close her eyes. She put her arms up, crossing them at the back of her head, displaying her chest. Big John shifted on his feet. Fiona grew nervous watching the focus deepen in his eyes.

Suddenly Michael appeared a few yards off from the others. Jane lowered her arms slowly, her demeanor changing. The smile left her face. For a few moments she did not move at all, the rain driving down on her. Michael was as still, his eyes on her.

"Mother," Fiona cried, opening the door.

Jane winced at the sound of Fiona's voice, then turned slowly and looked at her. She blinked, rain dripping from her lashes. She looked once more at the men, then fetched the basket, moving back toward the house, the men watching the back of her.

Eamon muttered something to Big John, who muttered in response, touching the heavy buckle of his belt. Martin laughed.

Jane pushed past Fiona and into the lavatory, trying to close her out, but Fiona pressed and struggled, preventing Jane from closing the door. "Why did you stand out there like that?" Fiona cried, hurt and anger sounding in her voice. Jane's eyes rose slowly to meet Fiona's, the shine on them cool like the shine on glass. A flame that had always lived in them for Fiona was not there, as if it had been snuffed out.

Stunned, Fiona let go of the door and Jane closed it. Fiona stood there awhile breathing hard before she went again into the other room and looked out the window. The others had moved off, but Michael was still standing there. He looked at Fiona, then turned away, disappearing behind the still standing barley.

Fiona could not keep things clear in her head. It was the field she focused on, almost gone. She imagined winter, that same ground hard with frost.

The turning circle of the year moved now with a terrible momentum.

From under her blankets Fiona watched Jane's shape across the room in her own dark bed. Exhausted, Fiona fought sleep. She kept thinking of the tiny blouse with the Presentation crest on it. The gray of it, the poorness.

She woke with a gasp. Jane's bed was empty. She got up and went into the kitchen, but Jane was not there.

Fiona could not feel her legs as she walked outside. It was as if she were floating, impelled by a will not her own toward the dim light in Michael's cottage. The door was ajar and opened easily as she pushed.

A garment lay on the floor. She heard fervent whispering, an intake of air. Two figures half in shadow moved on Michael's bed.

For a while Fiona ran, not certain where she was going. But she got too tired to keep running and found herself wandering like one of the orphan girls, dead before her time; one of the girls Jane had once fretted over, a girl whose life had been cut short. Fiona was near the beach. The moon rode on a bank of clouds, the water below it silver, streaming in and away.

She looked back at the blue color-washed house on the hill, no longer hers, the light she'd left on still glowing in the window. She yearned again to be the girl she'd been the summer now passed.

It was to Sister Delphine she went. It was to the nuns.

At Presentation she lay in a bed with a headboard like a warped, salt-eaten door. A room reserved for visiting priests. Unable to trespass into sleep, she wept, sweat on her face and neck and chest, her heart engorged. She was vomiting and someone held her head over a pan.

It was daylight, though overcast. Three nuns stood around the bed.

"She's in a terrible state," she heard one of them say.

"Her heart's worn down to a last thread."

She did not know if it was real or a dream. When they sopped her brow with a cool cloth, they murmured her name. Sometimes as they ministered to her, she thought she was with Moira and the two blond women again, being prepared for Beltane.

Jane came and went among the nuns like an apparition, her presence causing Fiona's heart to speed, causing her to turn her head from side to side until her scalp ached, her hair matted.

"I'm sorry," she heard Jane plead. Fiona banged the mattress with her fists. Jane crouched on her haunches in the corner of the room, her head in her hands, grieving like Mary Magdalene.

A priest came. Fiona felt an ice-cold crucifix pressed to her forehead.

*

Even after the fever broke, nuns streamed in and out. She heard Jane weeping in the hall, but refused to see her. Jane managed her way in anyhow, a devastated expression on her face. Before Fiona could even think, she hurled the ewer and basin from the nightstand at her. It made a terrible, crashing noise and the nuns came running in.

"Get her out!" Fiona cried. "Get her out!" And the nuns escorted Jane away. Fiona listened hard, hungry to hear penitence and suffering in Jane's weeping and protests. She knew that day as Jane's voice trailed off, echoing through the maze of corridors, that she'd never see or hear Jane again.

Ronan had offered to make arrangements for a flight from Limerick, but she was afraid to fly alone. She would make, instead, a transatlantic voyage from Cobh Harbor. He would meet her in New York and they would fly together to Albuquerque.

On the bus ride to Cobh, many fields were in midharvest, threshing still going on. Showers of grain poured out of chutes, the airborne chaff like particles still trying to settle after a blast.

From the deck of the ship she watched Ireland recede into the mist. She saw a single slim curragh moving north on the Greenland current.

"That frail thing'll be lost, surely," she heard a man say. She shivered. She was moving with the darkness of the year. And all the days of the voyage she spent outside on deck in the cold, closing her eyes, breathing in the wind and sea, remembering her days before Jane; her days of invisibility.

FOURTEEN

She'd been wrong about flying. She liked the sensation of rising above the earth and found herself wishing she could remain suspended in the sky, head resting on her seat back, gazing out into the stratosphere. The air on the plane was artificial and dry and buzzed faintly in her ear, yet she found a relief in its emptiness. She felt delivered somehow from danger, lifted above the fraught earth.

Ronan sat beside her leafing through a magazine he'd found in the seat back. When she'd first seen him at the pier before a backdrop of New York City skyscrapers, she thought him an uncanny figure, almost as out of place as she was. He wore a bolo tie with a chunk of polished onyx set in silver. "Southwestern jewelry, Navajo Indian," he would explain to her when her eyes kept leaving his to settle on it. He had other pieces, too, a heavy silver bracelet and a silver buckle on his leather belt. His cowboy boots were scuffed and beaten, deeply wrinkled at the insteps. Right away she'd felt him sensing her out. Her wire to him had sounded urgent, she'd thought in retrospect.

Yet he'd looked closely at her and knew somehow not to ask. She was still in wonder over that. His expression acknowledged that he saw something wrong, yet he left her miraculously alone.

He closed the magazine and said suddenly, "Are you thirsty?" as if it was a question he should already have asked.

"No."

He nodded. "The stewardess will come around soon anyhow. Maybe by then."

She smiled at his earnest wish to do for her. He smiled back, realizing, and colored slightly.

Once when she was sure he was looking away, she stole a curious glance at him. His red hair had less wave to it than she remembered, but was longer now by a few inches. One of his legs was crossed at an angle over the other so his ankle rested sideways on his knee, the sole of his boot facing her. He switched legs and she was faced with his threadbare knee. Through the tear in his jeans she saw his freckled skin. Sensing that he could feel her eyes on him, she looked away, turning her head to the window and the clouds.

*

Photographs had not prepared her for the panoramic vastness of New Mexico; or the oddness of the rockface, entire sides of a mountain glittering with mica, like shattered, silvery bits of glass.

Immense tracts of mesa ran for miles in every direction. Brush and piñon trees, flecks of yellow and purple wildflowers. The breadth and height of the landscape stunned her, the endlessness of the sky, the mountains in places vaulting up around them as Ronan wound along a dirt road. It was hot at midday, but Ronan explained that it would be cold at night. Very far off, impossible for Fiona even to gauge roughly how far on each horizon, was a range of mountains. She kept thinking they'd reach the ones they were headed toward, but for nearly an hour as they moved north from Albuquerque in Ronan's truck, the mountains remained on the horizon.

Dry earth hit the windshield. Tumbleweeds flew in the hectic force of the wind, cutting into the grill at the front of the truck. Wind that, when it was quiet, made a low, runneling cry like the howl of some fierce dog, maybe a coyote.

She found herself shying from the place, uneasy with it.

Light infused everything here. Even with her eyes closed, it leaked into her.

Ronan's house was reddish, resembling the foothills to the north. The walls, rounded masses, harmonized with the landscape, as if naturally occurring. A clean smell like new construction, white plaster and cut pine, filled the air. A huge fireplace under an undulating adobe hood seemed a primeval presence in the main room, the ashes of a recent fire thick on its blackened floor.

Ronan led her up a corridor into a separate wing of the

house where he had set up a bedroom for her with a wide bed and
a vast polished floor.

"I let Mrs. Bustamente choose the curtains and the bedspread," he said. They were muted tones of mauve and beige, an
abstract pattern of lines and squares. "You'll meet her later. She
comes in a few times a week to cook and clean."

This room had a pair of glass doors and she stepped outside
onto a patio area, overlooking some foothills covered with low
scrub-pine trees. Her head ached and she struggled to take a full
breath. He watched her, looking, she was sure, for her reaction to
the place. Again she felt him careful with her.

"It's fierce quiet here," she said. A crow cried in the distance and the echo of it made her melancholy. She rubbed her
forehead and her eyes with her hand. What she wanted most to
do was withdraw, to close the blinds and the curtains and to lie
down in the dimness.

"I'm exhausted," she said. After she was rested, she said,
maybe the scale of the place would not disorient her.

"It's hard to breathe at first," he said. "You're not used to
the elevation."

He put her suitcase on her bed, hesitated a moment, then
withdrew.

Her clothes, as she unpacked them, smelled of Ireland. She
ached reluctantly for rain.

Later when she came out of her room, Ronan was more formal
with her, shy. He nodded awkwardly when their eyes met. She
wondered if he was somehow disappointed with her.

He introduced Fiona to Mrs. Bustamente, who was in the
kitchen chopping onions for their evening meal. The small

brown woman nodded at her, then continued her work, a model of stern efficiency.

Before it got dark, Ronan walked Fiona down a mountain pathway overlooking a small Castilian village called Paseo de Sueños. The little earth houses had bright blue painted doorways and window frames. They walked up a dirt road that ended at the summit of a hill, the lit-up cliffs of a gorge to the west.

At the lip of the canyon he showed her the fossil of a seashell embedded in rock. Incredulous, she touched it with her fingertip, something like a scallop shell with fanning ridges.

"Traces of a bloody ocean," he said, and laughed.

The second night she spent in New Mexico, she dreamed she stood in the barley field.

She could hear the sounds of the Irish night. The tide. The distant barking of a dog. The wind brushing in the grain sounded like a woman's tremulous voice.

Michael came to her. There was no betrayal between them, only love. Love that made it difficult to breathe, her chest and lungs so tender and tight with it. He spoke to her in a language she worked to understand, the antiquated Irish he'd spoken at Beltane. By concentrating now she somehow understood. He was telling her about the impulse of life beginning under the valve that caused the heart to pump. That from that spot in the chest the root of the sex began and traveled down, a lit wire.

A change in the wind broke her concentration. She noticed that suddenly the barley was in stooks, the wind, multiple female voices now, captive within each barley huddle. Michael sighed, a sound with a soft ache in it. He showed her his swollen cock.

She went on her knees and took him in her mouth. He kept speaking his indecipherable words, broken now by sighs and moans of pleasure, but she could no longer understand the language, the increasing hysteria of the winds interfering with her ability to hear. She hated the voices and they grew louder and more frenzied.

With one hand on each of his naked hips, she took him as far back into her throat as she could. He held her head gently with both hands. She felt the tremor begin within him and drank him, the juice of him silty as if from the ocean floor. When he withdrew from her, a drop of semen was on the palm of her hand. She stared at it in the moonlight. Pearly in color and teeming with life. He lay bent into himself panting, and she awakened, smelling the sea.

She was confused, unable to remember why she'd exiled herself. How could anything have mattered enough to make her leave him? It felt irreparable and she lay smarting, unable to recapture the course of events.

Ronan had a job to do in Colorado at Mesa Verde, a site of ancient Indian ruins. He wanted Fiona to come, but she said she wanted to gain her bearings.

Alone, she ventured out only as far as the places she had walked with Ronan where the shrubs growing along the wash looked like plumes of gray-green smoke.

She went to look again at the fossilized seashell, touching it again, clearing bits of sand from its ridges, then stood and gazed at the distant edge of the canyon, an amphitheater of dry earth fired red by the sun. She imagined the train of the sea that had once been here slowly departing over the landscape.

*

A week after Ronan had left, Fiona asked Mrs. Bustamente to stay and eat supper with her. She searched for something to talk about.

"Will there be flowers in the spring?" Fiona asked.

"Not if it's a cold, dry winter," Mrs. Bustamente said in her characteristic unforthcoming manner. "We may not have any wildflowers in the spring."

The thought pained Fiona. She did not move for a few moments, staring at the food on her plate.

Mrs. Bustamente must have sensed the strong effect of her words on Fiona, because her tone was softer when she said, "You know, seeds can lie dormant in the dry grounds. Years could pass and they could still flower."

In restless half-sleeps Fiona thought she was sewing. Every seam she finished tore, her stitches always too soft, insufficient, and she struggled to fix them.

For the two weeks that Ronan was gone, the dreams burdened her. As the barley and the alder trees were prey to the furies of the wind, she and Michael sweat together like horses. She could see everything around them growing. Dog roses, the swamp blooming with bog lilies, overrun with them; verdure and bracken dense and green-black. Clotted with blood-colored berries. Chlorophyll inseparable from the rampant madness of sex. As they rolled together on the loam, she saw a single seed swell and complicate into the weighty baroqueness of a barley stalk. He was always there, inexhaustible. While she'd only just broken from him, she longed for him to take her again.

She'd wake startled and in a sweat, panting, on the verge of a rapture that would not come, but receded with consciousness.

*

Before she had left Ireland, she'd asked one of the nuns to get some of her things from Jane and send them on to her at Ronan's. A box of papers and letters and dress patterns, a scrapbook of photographs from school and a couple of favorite articles of clothing.

Ronan was back for one day when the package addressed to Fiona arrived. Jane had sent most of the things Fiona had asked for, but missing from the box was her nightgown and a light cotton blouse that Fiona had frequently worn that last summer. In a note to Fiona, Jane had written:

> Mrs. McGinty died the day after you left for America. Ned was at the door a week later with a marriage proposal. We will knock the fences down between our properties and have the biggest farm in Roundstone! We'll marry next month. Can you believe that I'll be buying my dress at the bridal shop in Galway?
>
> Please write, Fiona, and let me know how you're getting on.
>
> P.S. I'm keeping the blouse and the nightgown for you until I see you again.

She did not sign the letter.

It put Fiona out of spirits. She wondered if Jane had labored over the note, trying to sound casual. She thought of Michael, wondering what had happened to him, and found herself deluged with new dreams of him.

Ronan coaxed Fiona out of the house. He wanted her to see more of New Mexico. He yearned to spend time with her. He took her one day to Bandelier, ancient Indian caves reached by wooden ladders; and to a place called Camel Rock, where they sat on its summit in a high wind and gazed at an infinite distance of dry rock and mountain. On another day he took her to a network of caves and grottoes where shrines were set up to various local saints.

They descended a crude stairway in a cave, lamps on iron hooks impaled along a soft seam of rock running into darkness. The passage grew close and heavy with the smell of oil from the lamps, and they had to bow low to continue around the loop and descent where the cave opened suddenly onto the underground chapel of Nuestra Señora de la Soledad, whose statue stood in an alcove of flowstone.

In the close vault of the cave, Fiona could hear Ronan breathing. He ignited a match, the ensuing flame causing a riotous echo, and he lit a candle in the trembly, multilayered shrine and dropped a quarter into the metal offering box. He dipped his fingers in the pool and made the sign of the cross.

His face was intense, his head bowed.

Fiona disliked the elaborately dressed life-size figure, its face yellow and shiny and stern. The strangeness of it deepened her feeling of exile.

She closed her eyes and felt a moment of longing for Michael so intense she thought it would melt her. When she opened her eyes again, they filled, and the dwindling flames in the crooked, red-black votive glasses before the figure swam and blurred, then cleared as the tears ran down. Ronan watched her as she wiped her eyes with her fists.

"Fiona," he said, his soft voice echoing around them like a rushing of wings. Looking concerned, he approached her, but she moved away and began ascending the stairs.

*

They had to walk a half mile along narrow paths and back down a descent to where Ronan's truck was parked. Fiona kept pace a few yards ahead of him, stopping when unnerved by the darting of a lizard. Ronan watched her. She was embarrassed by her yearning and confusion. He caught up with her and placed his hand gently on her back so she started slightly, but as they walked, she was surprised by the comfort this afforded her.

It was then, in the time it took them to reach the truck, that she discovered the curious tranquilizing effect of the New Mexico sun. She imagined that the heat of it might erase her fretfulness, clean away the mildew and lichen of the darker, danker world. It occurred to her for the first time that it might have the power to obscure memory, to slow urgency, put her fecund urges to sleep.

And in those same moments the great refuge Ronan offered dawned on her.

At dinner that night she showed him photographs of the dresses she had made the previous summer.

The next evening he led her to one of the uninhabited rooms in the house. He had set up a sewing machine and a dressform for her. A ray of dusk light from the west-facing window lit them red. The dressform was not a type she had ever seen before, made of many adjustable flaps of metal, which gave it the appearance of womanly armor. The sewing machine was also odd, old-fashioned and delicate; black enamel with white filigrees of decoration across the arm. Accoutrements, a pedal and a buttonholer, sat on the floor at the foot of the dressform.

He shifted on his feet, watching her face.

"Thank you," she said, surprised by the hesitation she felt. She stared in from the doorframe but did not enter. The machine like a thresher, the mill, the shaft, and the chutes. The wheel.

"I hope you like these," he said, sensing her hesitation.

"I do. Thank you, Ronan." She met his eyes.

It was a mild evening and they ate outside under the porch light. Fiona found herself studying Ronan's complexion, marveling at how similar it was to her own. Cut from the same mottled satin, she thought. Skin so transparent, so quick to flush or burn, but close up, iridescent.

At the temples where his hair had begun to gray, it still held red like a faint wash of iodine. She wanted to hold a mirror up and look in it with him so they might search each other's face and their own; where they might discover other resemblances, things not so immediately noticeable.

She wanted to somehow reach out to him.

"We cast spells," she said.

"What?"

"My mother and I cast spells trying to bring you to us."

He looked at her cautiously a moment and did not breathe.

"We chanted your name. We sprinkled our tears on things you'd touched or left behind. A comb, a book of matches."

His look became intent, his eyes glinting. He got up from his chair and came to her, bending over, putting his arms around her.

During the day she'd go into the sewing room with vague intentions, thinking she might begin work on something simple. But she'd find herself unable to move.

In the hours of lethargy, she let the light coming directly in the big window warm her through so her eyes grew heavy. She gave herself over to the sun and felt it lifting her, chair and all, holding her aloft on the air of the room. She heard, as if from a great distance, the noise of dust hitting the windows.

At night she read. Turgenev, Tolstoy. European novels. Flaubert, Thomas Hardy, Henry James's novels set in Europe. Stories that took place in Italy, France. Stories dazzling with light. On the canals of Venice or the snow-covered Russian steppes under the evening star. She wanted the wideness of the world.

Ronan bought her a small beige Toyota truck with bad shock absorbers. She sped on the Española highway on her way into Santa Fe, where she took a variety of courses at the college: archery, landscape painting, astronomy. But she attended irregularly, opting to spend a day driving through the tiny northern New Mexico towns or into Pecos to be near the river. Sometimes she drove as far east as Villanueva, her little truck dancing jaggedly and noisily over the mountain roads.

PART THREE

THE LAND OF WOMEN

Verde viento. Verde ramas.
El banco sobre la mar.
Y el caballo en la montaña.

Green wind. Green branches.
The ship upon the sea.
And the horse on the mountain.
—FEDERICO GARCÍA LORCA

FIFTEEN

1972

A week after Carlos has gone to Ireland, Fiona awakens with more energy than usual. She walks restlessly around her house thinking she has to furnish the front room. She is tired of living in limbo.

She throws out things she's been ambivalent about keeping: an obsolete typewriter, a pair of her father's skis, hardly used, and a small bookshelf she now thinks of as an eyesore. She loads up her car and takes everything to the Salvation Army.

When she's there, a basket of scarves catches her eye and she looks through, coming across a frail panel of organza, a rectangle of it, about three feet by five. She can see by its condition that it was never used as a scarf or a shawl and is misplaced in this basket. Perhaps it had been a curtain once, she muses, though there is no sleeve for a rod. Along one of the four hems is a line of lace trim, complicated and dry; the color of bone. She buys it for twenty-five cents. At home, not knowing what to do with it, she lays it over the back of the wicker chair.

At night as she gets into bed and is about to turn off the lamp on her nightstand, she finds herself fixed on the white cotton curtain at her window. She thinks of the organza panel in the other room as its paler, more transparent twin. She has an impulse to sew the two together, the organza as a kind of overlayer to the cotton, an attenuated double, and hang them in front of the leaded-glass window in the main room.

She resists and turns off the light, though the thought keeps her awake. In the middle of the night she gets up and sews the organza directly over the cotton curtain, her hand moving with an excited rhythm. She puts up a rod over the leaded-glass window and hangs the curtain with its addition there. In places the glass panels are slightly separated from their frame and admit a breeze.

At dawn she awakens in the wicker chair and watches the two layers undulate together.

She is curious to find more old fabrics; fabrics with mysterious histories. In the vintage-clothing store on Marcy Street her attention is riveted by a basket in one corner filled with yards of old, fragile silk wound in a heap, a blue, reflecting brocade. The integrity of the weave is uneven and slightly frayed in places, and that excites her nearly as much as the swirling, wavelike motif. The fabric is shadowy and cold, blue-gray as air filled with thunderheads. The seawater of the Irish Atlantic before a rain.

She cannot resist going through the baskets, picking out more shattered, disintegrating silks, responsive to the opening and closing of the shop door. Bits of whitework and a tired lace that looks like a Limerick design: scalloped edges with an intricate floral center. And seven or eight crushed pieces of aqua, nylon gauze. She imagines the windy effect they might produce when sewn into layers.

When she gets home, she sits down at her kitchen table, sketching the contours of a woman's figure, her hand shaking so much she has to erase the lines many times, little flecks of gray eraser sticking to the indistinct skirts like dirty particles swirling in water.

She estimates as she cuts. This will not be a complicated construction; no arches or balustrades, just a single swathing circuit of fabric, manipulated slightly at the hip. Her urge is to achieve a kind of weightlessness in the unconstricted seams.

She leaves the windows open as she works, the fabric quivering and cold. The room is filled with the smell of rain and forlorn distance. Her heart jumps. She hears the keening of gulls. For long hours the muscles of her neck and shoulders ache. Her eyes water.

Late in the afternoon lightning flashes across the shadows of the room, followed by cracks of thunder and soft drifts of rain.

She lights a cigarette and stands back to look at the dress coming together. The wind through the screen rushes the skirt, which appears to tread the air. She shivers and closes the window.

She gasps as she turns, startled by the smoke from her cigarette floating near her shoulder.

The wind that night is turbulent, unseasonably cold. She looks out and sees the shadows of leaves shaking on the adobe wall, half lit by the moon.

She remembers a night when she was small and had asked her mother, "Who are the dead?"

Jane had hesitated. "They're us. That's all. Our ancestors. Our friends."

"Why do they come back?"

"They're tied to places and to people."

Years later, in the blue color-washed house, when Michael had told her and Jane the story of his father, he had said, "The dead and the living do not lead such separate lives."

She thinks of that last summer, she and Jane eclipsing each other, being swallowed in the other's light or darkness; traveling the lost places within each other.

It had always been so, her own edges blurred painfully with Jane's. When she was four or five years old, they'd argued once— over what, she can't recall—it had been terrible and felt to Fiona that the world would end, so much had it seemed that nothing could make things right again. She'd lain in her room in near darkness crying, and after a little while Jane had come and they lay entangled, the hurt slowly healing.

She looks at the photographs of Jane on the beach of the Spanish ships and marvels again as she always has at the strangeness of the light.

It had been that same night when she was small, after they reconciled, that she told Jane she remembered the day the pictures were taken, and Jane had told her that it was impossible.

But it was something Fiona had felt certain of. "It's my first memory!" she had insisted, and Jane had laughed and kissed her.

Looking now into Jane's kindling eyes, eyes that extend the softest of invitations, Fiona feels that certainty again. She remembers being drawn toward Jane and descending upon her as any homeless soul all adrift might be drawn toward such warmth.

Uncanny air blows through her screen, wet as the Greenland current.

All spring and summer she makes dresses. She makes them breathlessly, cutting the thread on one and beginning another. She gives herself again to the memories of that last Irish summer. Michael's tongue, the smell of his skin. His cock, not to be deterred. And for a while, as she reclaims her powers as a seamstress, it is Michael at the forefront of her thoughts.

Her body unfurls as she works her silks: charmeuse, taffeta, brocade; heavy cream or light crepe silk. She wants dark or deep colors: crimsons and bronzes. Forest greens, ambery golds. She has lost interest in wide skirts and constricting seams, and seeks out companion fabrics more and more weightless, transparent.

Some days she sews with nothing on, her pulses galloping. It amazes her, how love remains, hiding in her skin, flooding up from the cells as she works. The pleasure costs her. It is excruciating to feel the depths of her hunger.

The dresses that come forth from these hours are filled with electricity. The simplest among them, a statuesque sienna brown, almost Greek looking in its line, emits loneliness. Though all are narrow in the skirt, Fiona has given herself over to her passion for the unusual or voluminous sleeve: some with dropped shoulder yokes, smocked and tight at the upper arm, then ballooning out over the forearm; or bishop sleeves, wide sweeping bells with fitted lace undersleeves. Each dress suggesting mood, desire. Some, Fiona thinks, are misfits, discontents. Some she endows, like the curtain, with a less visible twin attached as a layer. Giving the impression of being half there and half not, its own apparition preceding it.

Her front room slowly fills, peopled now in dresses, standing on forms or displayed on hangers.

Near summer's end she has grown impatient with cloth. She yearns for a damper medium and finds herself thinking of the petals of the sacred datura, which maintain liquid in their very fibers. She collects them from the mesa up the long dirt road off the Española highway where Ronan once took her and obsessively attempts to make a dress she has to water like a plant; a moist, velvety dress with a fleeting life of its own.

Stitching carefully, a living fabric of petals, she gradually comes to know that this desire she feels is larger than Michael, bleeding out beyond him. And though it is his face she's been seeing, she finds in this hour that it isn't there. The eroticism feels diffused, on the air around her. It is as if she were looking at a photograph beginning to develop in Ronan's darkroom water; a shadow coming slowly toward her. Gradually, a different man's face finds clarity and appears.

Sixteen

One late afternoon in September, Fiona walks to the plaza where the Fiesta de Santa Fe is in full swing.

Crowds move among the various booths, the air smelling of cotton candy and sopaipillas.

In a band shell erected on the flagstones under ancient cottonwoods, a mariachi band, five stocky, sombreroed men in red and gold velvet, plays a lively serenade. "*Amoroso,*" two men sing in a high-pitched cry. *"Amoroso,"* punctuated by the harmonic sputtering of horns.

When the music stops and the sparse, chaotic cheering from the crowd dies, Fiona hears the clopping hooves of horses on Palace Avenue. High on horseback, both wearing the tri-cornered helmet and heavily ruched doublets of conquistadores, are the two Aragon brothers, José on a gray horse and Carlos on an Appaloosa.

She feels a twinge, wondering how long he's been back. In May, a few weeks after he'd left for Ireland, Fiona had received a postcard from Smerwick Harbor on the Dingle Peninsula: *Fiona— All things in place. We dive tomorrow. X, Carlos*

Another postcard had come in June: *Unrelenting wind and rain. Still I'm diving each day. Carlos*

But no word since. When the horses come to a stop, Carlos looks down and sees her in the crowd. Fiona meets his eyes and then smiles slightly at the way he is rigged up. He descends from the saddle and stands beside the horse, who also peers at Fiona.

She can see now a blush risen under the brown of his skin, and she finds herself moved by his embarrassment. He shuffles like the horse before approaching her. He looks as if he does not know what to say, so she helps him.

"What did you find in Ireland?"

She thinks from his expression that he has come back unsatisfied.

The pause is awkward so Fiona shifts her attention to the horse, stroking the velvet of its nose with her palm. It has dark brown eyes with yellow-white lashes. Its response to her touch is an exquisite combination of gentleness and unease.

"When did you get back?"

"Three days ago," he says.

From horseback, José confers with one of the mariachis,

who in turn speaks to the other musicians. They all glance at Carlos.

"They're waiting for you," Fiona tells him.

When Carlos turns, José gestures for him to follow. Carlos remounts, the color still up in his face. His horse's ears go up. It opens its mouth against the bit, taking nervous steps sideways.

"Wait for me here," Carlos says to Fiona from the saddle.

The mariachis begin a loud serenade, and as the two horsemen parade around the plaza, girls in red fiesta skirts and peasant blouses cry out in time to the music and children throw confetti. When Carlos and José come full circle, the air is frenetic with jubilation.

Fiona joins Carlos and they walk up Palace Avenue, away from the festivities, Carlos leading the horse by the reins. She wants to ask him again about Ireland but feels careful, sensing disappointment.

They are quiet for a few moments before he asks, "Have you ever been in a boat on the Blasket Sound?"

"No."

"It's four square miles of hazardous ocean. A calm sea can break into mountains of waves in minutes. And the weather was against me. The way it was against the Armada ships. Storms and rough water."

Fiona feels upset with the Irish weather, vaguely responsible for it.

When they reach the Paseo de Peralta, Carlos stops. "Do you want to ride up to Tesuque with me now?"

She smiles. "On the horse?"

"Yes. Her name is Flurry." He points out the tiny dots of white in the brown areas of her coat.

He mounts, then reaching down for her hand tells her to

put her right foot in the stirrup. When she does, he pulls her up. They ride up the Paseo and turn on the road to Tesuque, the afternoon beginning to deepen toward evening. She is pressed to his back, her arms around his waist. Secretly, she fingers the rough, rippled cloth of his doublet and the cold metal hooks that hold the garment together.

When they reach a network of dirt roads, the horse begins to canter.

"She's anxious to get home," Carlos says to Fiona over his shoulder.

The horse moves quickly through a maze of thick paths and up an ascent to Carlos's house. The tamarisks look taller, fuller, and have lost their pink with summer's end. After they dismount, Carlos settles the horse in her corral, where she drinks from the trough. He breaks apart a compacted bushel of alfalfa and throws it in to her. As he saunters toward Fiona, he tosses the tricornered helmet into the small shed where alfalfa is stored and slams the little wooden door shut on it. He is still embarrassed by the garb, she thinks. He smiles but does not meet her eyes as he pulls the hooks loose on the doublet.

She steps down after him into his front room, full of late-afternoon shadows.

"Do you want something to drink?" he asks her.

"Sure."

He peers into the cold brightness of the refrigerator. "Water or beer?"

"Beer."

She hears him open a drawer, rifle through cutlery, and open the beers.

Missing the horseback ride and the feeling of her body

pressed to his, she sits in the worn leather chair where she imagines he often sits.

He hands her a bottle, then sits on the Taos bench, resting his head all the way back against the wall. Dust motes swirl in the late sun, coming through a west-facing window. The house looks neglected, unswept. Carlos's suitcase lies open on his bedroom floor, clothes in a heap, unfolded.

"I *did* find *La Alma Verde,* Fiona."

"You did?" she gasps.

"But I lost her."

"How?"

"Well, in the research Gaston had done, he discovered documents from a ship called the *San Juan.* We found out that *La Alma Verde* was a cargo vessel, a small ship loaded with horses and guns, and that the crew of the *San Juan* saw her go down in the Blasket Sound. We even know the date. September twenty-first, 1588."

"Amazing," Fiona says, sitting forward. She gazes at his profile as he remains with his head back, takes in his presence.

"Two hours before daybreak she was spotted with her lantern burning. She foundered suddenly and it had been very dramatic. Horses and men overboard, struggling in the sea. It was in deep water that she sank, a league and a half from land. One man was sighted trying to save himself, holding on to broken planks. They tried to reach him but he disappeared in the fog. I'm certain that was Enrique Salazar."

"It must have been," Fiona says softly.

"We gathered a good crew and did something called a weighted line, which is towed behind the diving boat, with myself and Gaston hanging on the end. The boat steered a prearranged course toward Blasket Island anchorage. Gaston and I were in the water about fifteen minutes or so when we spotted a cannon, clearly visible, lying there in a smooth esplanade of seafloor and a mound of rubble where three cannonballs were embedded between stones. I thought my heart came out my mouth. At the same time the current was getting fierce, so we couldn't tie our line to the find and we had to make an emergency ascent to signal the boat to stop. A sea mist had fallen, so one of the men in our crew, Henri, who had been stationed on land to watch the boat's course, lost sight of us. With the mist we had no landmarks at all to tell us where we'd found the wreck, and the sea was too violent then to go back down. I thought we were closer to Beginish Island, but Gaston thought we were closer to the Great Blasket. We had no marker buoy, and because of the heavy sea and the uncertainty of our position, we couldn't give up a life jacket to improvise one. We set an eastern course and reached the mainland cliffs, hugging the shore and reaching the jetty at Dunquin." He sits forward, his elbows on his knees, and sighs.

"Over the next weeks we did the towed searches again and again, trying to re-create the conditions of the original dive, but we couldn't find it. We combed the water relentlessly. The crew began to lose interest. In Flannery's, the pub where we drank at night in Dunquin, we heard about another excavation being planned. Another Armada ship, the *Santa Anita,* was suspected of being twenty miles or so south near Slieve Miskish. A lot of my crew left and joined that party. They found the ship immediately and tons of relics. Gaston talked me into coming one day on a dive with the crew.

"The men were clearing boulders from the seabed, moving things about, unearthing things from beneath the sand and the kelp. Gaston found coins, pieces of eight. Later he was so excited. He said that every time he found a relic, it was like his hand was closing over history. So many things were found. Iron ingots, cannons and cannonballs, small arms, coins. One man brought up a silver candlestick. But *La Alma Verde* . . ." Carlos shakes his head.

She takes a drink of beer and, putting the bottle down, feels the euphoric sensation it induces. Moisture runs in rivulets down the bottle, the gold liquid catching the last of the daylight. The whole house softly hums with Carlos, in sync with him.

"At night in the pub, Gaston talked about the history of Europe, about Philip II. When he was drunk, he said absurd things about fighting Protestantism. He talked about Mary, Queen of Scots, like he was in love with her. He was happy to be excavating any Armada ship. He'd lost his passion for *La Alma Verde.* We argued and parted ways.

"But I continued to go out looking for my ancestor's ship. A few men who had been unable to sign on with the other expedition stayed with me. The weather was getting worse but I dove anyhow. I spent eight hours at a time, thirty feet under in water so icy it numbed me to the core and made my sinuses ache. I pushed myself, testing my endurance, coming to believe that I must suffer with the same intensity that Enrique Salazar did.

"I'd been diving with just the two hired men for more than a month, fighting a kind of growing despair. One afternoon, after a long day underwater, I came up feeling defeated. Every muscle ached and I could hardly move. The two men went under to bring up the gear and I was taking off my tanks. I knew I was too exhausted to dive again. I just knew I couldn't and that I'd come to the end of the search.

"That's when I saw them." He paused for a moment before continuing, "A heavy mist had come up and through it I saw a little boat with three figures in it, rocking on the waves. It came closer and closer and I could see that they were women, though their faces were never clear. Through a tear in the mist, I saw one of the women's hands. A relaxed hand resting on her knee. It looked as if she had a dark long skirt on. But the hand was the only thing I saw vividly, clear down to the tiny droplets on the skin. I felt as if I were staring at the hand a long time waiting for them to come closer. But the boat withdrew. The mist lifted suddenly and there was no sign of them. The two men climbed aboard with the gear and I asked them if they'd seen the shadow of a small boat on the water. They said they hadn't. It was after that that reason seemed to abandon me. I was ill that night and spent the next week in the hospital.

"When I was well I stayed a few days more walking the shores, raking the water with my eyes for the boat with the women, wondering if I'd really seen it."

The shadow of a tamarisk branch sways across the last of the daylight on the wall and Carlos watches it. "The past is a separate country," he says.

In the moments of silence that follow, evening deepens in the room. Fiona daydreams Carlos searching in the green twilight of deep water, moving through pinnacles and shingles. She imagines him coming across an iron ingot half-buried. Pulled up from under the sand, it reveals itself to be a network of iron, the headboard of a bed. The bed Enrique Salazar slept in. The bed of nightmares, of nurturing. The bed of lovemaking.

Is it about geography, she wonders, the places where myth and reality touch? How do you search out a myth? Where does it live?

The room is dark now but Carlos does not reach for the lamp on the table between them. He sits with his hand shielding his eyes, looking within himself at some dimming horizon. The shadows just beyond his shoulder have taken on a velvety texture. The idea of the three women seems real to Fiona in this moment and inspires in her a deepened feeling of tenderness toward Carlos, a milky, languid sensation that moves in a wave over her flesh and becomes palpitatingly carnal. He is beautiful sitting there in his loneliness.

Fiona touches his forearm, wishing now that he might ask her to stay, that it is her turn to offer balm against his suffering, but he does not respond. There is a heaviness to him. After a moment, she withdraws her hand. With some secret sense that perceives what her outer senses do not, she feels the pulsing of his heart all around her.

As he drives her back into Santa Fe, the mood stays with him.

"Did you ever find a mirror for your dress shop?" he asks, a flatness in his voice.

"No, no. I haven't even looked."

"Why not?"

"I'm so disorganized. I guess I'm putting things off."

"Why?"

"I've been sewing a lot. Making dresses. But I can't imagine selling them."

"Can I come in and see?"

"There's a clutter in there now."

He shrugs his shoulders.

She hesitates, then agrees.

He parks near the curb in front of her house and follows her through the gate and across the threshold into the main room.

"Christ," he whispers as she switches on the light. Some dresses hang over him like angels about to descend. He moves through them, touching them, admiring.

"You made all of these?"

"Yes." She laughs nervously. "Since I met you in the spring."

"All of them?"

"Yes."

"How many are there?"

"Twenty-one."

"And you don't want to sell them?"

She sighs and shakes her head. "The thought upsets me."

He bends close to a dress of dark gold brocade, studying the embroidery on the bodice. "I can understand that."

He looks at each one thoughtfully and with a penetrating eye. It unnerves Fiona. She has a fleeting thought that one of the dresses might do something suddenly to make her ashamed.

She laughs to herself at the irrationality of the thought and looks at them anew, moved and confused by their eccentricities.

The melancholy lifts from Carlos as he moves through the dresses, a chaos of ribbons, cloth swatches, and thread littering the floor. A certain restrained vitality has returned to his physique. Though he is still guarded with her, his eyes flash to hers once and she detects an enormity of admiration.

"This one looks like she wants to venture into the world," he says, pointing to a long, Empire-waisted dress with a tiny fraught embroidery on its bodice. The dress leans forward, leading from the chest.

He stops before another, a dark one, the threads of its embroideries bleeding out of their outlines suggesting quivering auras around the leaves and flowers. Its shoulders slope, exuding disappointment. *"Lejana y sola,"* he says thoughtfully. *"Piensa que el mundo es chiquito."*

"And this one," he says, stopping before a loose, creamy dress with an undercurrent of tension at its waist and a neckline bordered with roses made of twists of silk. *"Los pétalos de lujuria,"* he says, and grazes the sleeve with his fingertip.

She feels a rush, remembering his hot mouth, his hands on her waist as she moved over him. She turns away, goes into the kitchen on the pretense of getting a drink of water.

When she comes back, he is sitting in the wicker chair looking around the room. He is quiet a few moments before he says in a slow voice, "I could help you with the shop. I could polish this floor for you and touch up the plasterwork on the walls." He points to the cracks near the ceiling that Victor Jaramillo never got to. "I can put up some racks for you if you want. It wouldn't be difficult. And some of these dresses you probably want to keep on their forms to give the full effect of them. You know, to display them."

She looks in his eyes, hoping to meet with a certain softness, but he is keeping a distance with her.

He looks around at the room and seems to be making calculations in his mind. "I was thinking, I could put in little elevations, like small stages to stand some of the forms on."

"Well, I'd pay you, of course," she says.

He gives her a stern, insulted look.

He arrives early the next morning with a thermos of coffee and his tools.

She helps him move all the dresses and forms into her sewing room, then asks if she can help him further.

"No, you go on with the things you have to do. I'll let you

know if I need you." His manner hasn't softened much from the previous night.

She decides she should do what she's been putting off: finish the paperwork and take it to Mr. Vigil. She fills in the spaces on the form that she'd left blank. When she comes to the space that asks for the name of the shop, she dawdles. It's something she's never given enough consideration to. She hears Carlos mutter something in Spanish in the next room.

She writes *La Alma Verde* in the blank space.

At the end of the week, Fiona helps Carlos move the dresses and forms into the newly finished shop. She goes into the kitchen to make them some coffee, leaving Carlos to repair a loose bolt on one of the dress racks.

After she turns the burner on under the water, she goes to ask him if he wants something to eat with it.

He is standing before one of the dresses that he whispered to the first night, the dark one that Fiona thinks looks disappointed. His head down, he holds the sleeve. He is far away, unaware of her presence.

His reverence for her dresses confounds her. At moments these past days, she's felt he's been more at their service than hers, more cordial to them than to her.

Looking at them all standing now in the shop, they feel separate from her, each complete in itself, like impatient daughters ready to go their own ways. Sensing her presence, Carlos looks up and holds her eyes. He drops the sleeve that he's been holding, then looks around the room. "They're facets of you, Fiona. All of them. They're your avatars."

Her heart is wild. She wonders why his words, given in a spirit of admiration, cause her pain. And then she knows that it is because he can see her, the strangeness of her, the isolation. When he looks at them, he knows them to be the beautiful monuments to her unlived lives.

The night before Fiona opens her dress shop, she prepares early for bed. She is in her nightgown when Carlos knocks on the door.

"I have a surprise for you," he says. "Come outside." She looks at the sky, the clouds massing for a downpour. The house is dim except for her bedroom light down the hall.

She goes out barefoot and finds the restored statue of the girl in green set like the shop's guardian inside the gate, heavily gessoed and sealed so the first patters of rain hit and bead up before rolling off.

"Carlos. You didn't have to give her to me."

"She belongs here," he says, holding her eyes.

She touches his face with the palm of her hand, then leads him inside into the shop full of dresses.

She lifts her nightgown and puts his palm on her naked hip. "You're so soft," he utters. She wonders if he hears the dresses whispering; if he knows about the commotion he has started among them. She slides her flattened palms up under his shirt to feel the hot satin of his skin.

When the dresses are gone, she thinks, they will remember him in his nakedness.

They make love in a tender delirium on the floor, while she says, "Tell me about the light on the Gulf of Cadiz. Tell me about the weather."

But instead, he tells her again about Betazos by the sea where Enrique Salazar remained until he died, peering always north toward Ireland; the place where Spain and Ireland resolve into a single rainy place. As she feels the floor swimming beneath them, she sees the green stormy light he describes and imagines a dress that is mostly condensation; layers of mist and mesh rising from skirt and sleeves like steam from a humid sea.

ABOUT THE AUTHOR

REGINA MCBRIDE is the author of *The Nature of Water and Air* and the recipient of fellowships from the National Endowment for the Arts and the New York Foundation for the Arts. Her poems have been widely published in literary journals and magazines, and her book of poetry *Yarrow Field* won an American Book Series Award. She grew up in Santa Fe, New Mexico, and lived for a time in Ireland before moving to New York City, where she now resides with her husband and daughter.

This is her second novel.

THE LAND OF WOMEN

DISCUSSION POINTS

1. Consider the language in the first paragraph. What do you learn about the characters and about the story?

2. Look at the opening quote, "Begin a voyage across the clear sea, / If you would reach the Land of Women." Recount the story of the Land of Women. What does it mean to you? Discuss whether it's a man's fantasy. Why do you think Regina McBride uses it here for her title?

3. What are your early impressions of Fiona? Think about her life story and discuss what kind of person she is. How does her relationship with her mother define her?

4. What are your impressions of Jane? What kind of relationship do mother and daughter have? Consider the openness of their relationship, and discuss which one is more maternal.

5. What is significant about the story of "the bog girl"? What was she holding in her hands? Why does the story fascinate Fiona? Do you think there is a connection, symbolic or otherwise, among "the bog girl," the orphanage, and Fiona.

6. Discuss McBride's use of memory. For example, consider the smell of Jane on the first page, Fiona's abandonment when Jane left to be with Ronan in Chapter 2, and Fiona's tactile feeling of sex in Chapter 15—"It amazes her, how love remains, hiding in her skin, flooding up from the cells . . ." How do these memories inform and enhance the story? Share some of your memories that bubble up from nowhere when you smell, hear, or see something unrelated. How does reading about the memories of others stir your own?

7. Were you surprised at the historic Irish/Spanish intermingling? Why is Fiona attracted to Carlos? Discuss Fiona's first impression of him as he "calmly ministers to the battered figure" of a girl from a sunken ship. Could that also describe Fiona? What is symbolic about the small statue, considering, for example, that there are Celtic knots on the bodice of the figure's dress?

8. Why is Carlos fascinated by the tale of the Land of Women? Why is he attracted to Fiona? Discuss the fact that his ancestor claimed

to have visited the Land of Women and the "coincidence" that Fiona is Irish. When she and Carlos are alone in the basement of the antique shop, Fiona says of the rain, "It's like the sea air . . . has crossed a continent to find me." What does this mean?

9. If you know the *Odyssey*, how does it relate to the tale of the Land of Women? What relevance does it have to this story?

10. Consider the last paragraph of Chapter 4, "She gets up . . . visible on the overhanging cliff." What does the image represent? How do the various components of the picture incorporate critical elements of the story? If you recall other photographs throughout the book, how are they used to illuminate and deepen the scenes where they appear?

11. What do you make of the Giantess—the wedding dress that Jane kept? Why couldn't Jane part with it? What does it represent? What is the history of the dress, and what is the symbolism of its end?

12. How does sewing connect Jane and Fiona? Discuss the suitability of sewing as both mother and daughter's avocation for this story. Why is dressmaking thought of as "inseparable . . . from womanliness" (last paragraph of Chapter 5)? What are some of the things that sewing metaphorically represents? Look at and discuss the description of the dresses in Chapter 12, "each dress . . . carried and laid like invalids across backseats. And the wedding gown laid out . . . as if in a dead faint."

13. What is Fiona looking for when she goes to Carlos's shop in Chapter 8? Discuss the paragraph "In a glass box . . . held in suspension." What are its different levels of meaning? Consider what is going on when Carlos brings Fiona to his house and he reads his relative's diary to Fiona. How does McBride convey the sensuality and attraction between them? When they have sex, what does it mean that Fiona is "reclaiming the skelligs and western cliffs of Ireland. The beaches and the rocky points, all feel, at this moment, inseparable from her?"

14. How does McBride describe Fiona's sexual awakening? Is Michael real or imaginary? Share your reaction to the Mayday celebration of Beltane. What does it mean? What forces Fiona to leave her mother, and Ireland?

15. The dresses inspire the men in Fiona's and Jane's lives. Upon seeing the Giantess, Michael says, "It's desire fuels such a creation. It's passion." Carlos reveres Fiona's dresses, calling them her "avatars" . . . the beautiful monuments to her unlived lives. What do you make of Michael's and Carlos's reactions? What do they see in the dresses that gives them more insight into these women?

16. Why does it take Carlos's prompting for Fiona to open her shop? Do you think the shop becomes the Land of Women?

17. What would your answer be to Fiona's unasked question near the book's end, "Is it about geography, she wonders, the places where myth and reality touch. How do you search out a myth? Where does it live?" Is this the central question of *The Land of Women*? Discuss whether or not you think McBride has successfully answered this question with this story, and why.

Q&A with Regina McBride

Q. You capture a wonderful feeling for the Irish language and Ireland. You create poetry out of place names like Athlone, Roundstone, Doolough, Cashel Bay. Is your family Irish?

A. Yes, my family is Irish American. I have always loved to look at maps, place-names suggesting the mystery and particularness of a town or a city. I love language, the sounds, the rhythms, the tastes of words. Certain names seem to conjure the very weather of a place; its landscape or architecture.

Q. What inspired you to create a story around the tale of the Land of Women?

A. The mythic, paradisal isles of the Irish west have such evocative names: The Holy Isles, the Place of Apples, the Land of Women. In reading the ancient texts about these isles their nature remains elusive. It is difficult to know in the atmosphere of such magic, what is real and what is illusion. Enrique Salazar's story and the "land of women" in my novel are not out of the old texts, but something I created myself. Myths have a kind of dreamlike flexibility. They almost ask to be reconfigured and transformed.

Q. It seems that Fiona and her shop become a contemporary Land of Women. Is this what is happening?

A. I do think the dress shop becomes, for both Fiona and Carlos, a "land of women," a sort of unexpected paradise where the two come fully together. Enrique Salazar's story is, I feel, a very erotic story. On the surface it may seem like a male fantasy because Enrique Salazar has three women lovers, but if you look closely, he has come into an intensely female place filled with mysterious secrets. The three enigmatic women have chosen him and brought him there when he is in a deeply vulnerable state, having suffered profoundly and come close to death.

I think the myth suggests that paradise costs; it is not a place a man can enter wrecklessly. Enrique Salazar's nature is searching and self-reflective, something his descendant Carlos has in common with him. An attitude of reverence is required, the attitude that Carlos brings with him into Fiona's dress shop. He surrenders in a sense to the mystery of Fiona, puts himself at her service.

Q. You also have a remarkable talent for conveying the particulars of sewing. Are you someone who sews and knows fabrics?

A. Fabric is so sensual, and I have always been fascinated by costume and how one can be transformed by a dress. When I was younger, I used to do elaborate embroideries on all my boyfriends' denim jackets, but I do not sew. It has always fascinated me, though, and I have many books about sewing. There is some marvelous language around needlecraft.

Q. With all of the connotations associated with sewing, how did you figure out that you wanted sewing to be a prominent "thread" of the story?

A. From the time I was eleven or twelve, I was enamored of Tennyson's poem "The Lady of Shallot," the passionate, imprisoned woman whose tapestries were cloth-and-thread renderings of her deepest yearnings.

In Greek mythology sewing and spinning are often about powerful female magic; about generation and regeneration. The Three Fates come foremost to mind. Clotho, the spinner who spins the thread of life; Lechesis, who assigns each person a destiny; and Atropos, "she who can not be turned," who carries "the abhorred shears" and cuts the thread at death.

I'd say that dresses are a kind of obsession with me. Like many girls, when I was little I thought my dolls were alive. But I was also suspicious that my dresses were alive. I watched them on the clothesline or hanging in my closet. I did not think they were evil like I sometimes suspected my dolls were. The dresses seemed almost pensive and faraway. Sometimes sad or angry.

Q. Was the Giantess an outcome of the story of the unmarried woman making wedding dresses, or did the idea of the Giantess come first? It's a perfect child's nightmare, on top of everything else, by the way.

A. I think the fascination with the swollen, overblown dress came first. I used to look at some of the monstrous dresses that Spanish Infantas wore in sixteenth- and seventeenth-century paintings. They were eerily large, at once beautiful and terrifying. Such garments seem to transcend a dress's nature and become something more. Wearing it, a woman must navigate the world carefully and self-consciously. Such a dress confers royalty upon its wearer, making her into something mythic, something to be revered, even as it handicaps her, inhibiting mobility.

Q. Fiona's father is a photographer, and you are very deliberate about your use of photographs throughout the book. What do photographs mean to you as a writer, and how do you decide when and where to use them in a story?

A. Photographs of my parents from long-ago times have always moved me. I remember one of my father in his youth, sitting in an armchair with his legs crossed, casually smoking a cigarette, smiling and looking into the lens like the world was his oyster; and one of my mother as a girl laughing with incredible vitality, her head thrown back. One can stare and stare at a photograph, contemplate it and muse and feel awe.

The photographs in the novel "appeared," surfacing constantly as I wrote the story. I had to edit them down, organize them so they were there only in the most significant places.

When I was small we had a box camera, square and black like a house with two small, cloudy windows and no door. My father stunned me when he told me that a camera had a memory. I thought then that touching a certain button sent the message that it should "remember" that particular moment, which it somehow captured and miniaturized. I believed there were tiny rooms inside where it stored the pictures.

Q. The mother-daughter relationship in *The Land of Women* is complex and difficult. Jane, the mother, separates herself from her child little by little, eventually creating an irreparable situation. How did you decide to keep Fiona from being unmoored, which would have been one possible outcome of her difficult home life?

A. After Fiona returns from Beltane and Jane tells her about her early relationship with Ronan, they have a moment of deep closeness: "In Jane's arms Fiona felt herself going back. Back before Michael. Before Ned. Back to just the two of them. Some quiet, shared darkness. Some noise of water and membrane."

That shared connection between the two of them was always there throughout Fiona's girlhood, at the bottom of everything. This love is what kept Fiona "moored" until that final summer. And it is that same feeling of connection that Fiona eventually returns to at the end of the book. This pure, original feeling between them.

Q. Writing about sex is notoriously difficult, yet you handle it very naturally. It's also rare to see female sexuality from a woman's point of view. Was this important for you to do? Was it a big challenge?

A. I don't find writing about sex "notoriously difficult," although I have heard this often said. I love to write about sensory experience, and what is more profoundly sensory? The nuanced, emotional feelings sex lets loose in us inspire poetic description. Yes, it is deeply important to me to write about female sexuality because it is such rich, expansive territory. I think a character's sexuality is inseparable from her passion and her yearning and her capacity to love, and a direct expression of her nature.

Q. What captivates you about Fiona's question near the book's end—"Is it about geography, she wonders, the places where myth and reality touch. How do you search out a myth? Where does it live?"

A. I am very interested in the conflict between the external mythos of a place and the internal, personal mythos, or the beloved place as it lives in the imagination.

Many writers deliberately exile themselves from the place they come from and need to write about. Though it is painful, longing is a romantic state and good for many writers.

I haven't been back to Ireland in twenty-two years and am a little afraid to return there because it has taken on such mythic and emotional importance for me. The place as I remember it has alchemized with my own imaginings and yearnings about it.

Q. Are you working on another novel? And, if so, what's it about?

A. The working title of my new novel-in-progress is "The Marriage Bed." It takes place in Ireland in the early 1900s, a darker, more epic novel than *The Land of Women*. The story is told through the voice of a woman, Deirdre O'Breen, who has married into a family with a heavy, oppressive legacy, which causes her husband to suffer and to live, in a sense, as a "divided self." One of these selves she thinks of as "The Beloved," while the other she lives in strife with.

Deirdre is the mother of two teenage daughters whose dawning womanhood and struggle to break from her arouse uneasy memories from her own girlhood on the primitive Great Blasket Island in Ireland's western sea (a place that became uninhabited in the 1950s).

"Regina McBride writes in a shimmering and hypnotic prose...
The Nature of Water and Air
casts an undeniable spell."
—Emily White, *The New York Times Book Review*

0-7432-0323-2 • $13.00

TOUCHSTONE
A Division of Simon & Schuster
A VIACOM COMPANY

www.simonsays.com